"Ma

Nicholas had never f... his voice did not refle...

Once seated, he forced the reluctant words off his tongue. "Miss Dempsey, I would be honoured if you will be may wife."

Claire looked him directly in the eyes. "Do you not desire even a modicum of affection from your spouse, my lord?"

"No, Miss Dempsey, I do not," he said, his cultured tones soft, yet firm. "I've chosen you because you possess several qualities I admire. I feel it possible we might deal tolerably well together. If that is, you agree to be my wife."

Silently, Calire bade goodbye to all her hopes for the future. She turned to him with her head held high. "Yes, my lord," she murmured. "I will be your wife."

"You've made me a very happy man, Miss Dempsey."

And you, my lord, she thought with burning resentment, have made me the most wretched of all women.

Books by Janeane Jordan

HARLEQUIN REGENCY ROMANCE
66–THE SCHEME OF THINGS

KENTON'S COUNTESS

JANEANE JORDAN

Harlequin Books

TORONTO • NEW YORK • LONDON
AMSTERDAM • PARIS • SYDNEY • HAMBURG
STOCKHOLM • ATHENS • TOKYO • MILAN
MADRID • WARSAW • BUDAPEST • AUCKLAND

With love to my family and friends
Your support and encouragement helped
make a dream come true

Published June 1992

ISBN 0-373-31176-1

KENTON'S COUNTESS

CHAPTER ONE

A DAMNED BEASTLY BUSINESS, this quest for an acceptable wife, thought Nicolas Shea, fifth Earl of Kenton. 'Twas a quest which involved a removal to London each Season to survey the new crop of debutantes, and entailed a succession of tedious balls, endless routs and musicales, and—horrors—a parade of insipid misses forever being thrown at his head. In years past, he'd cast a jaundiced eye upon the misses and the games they played to capture his attention. This year, however, circumstances beyond his control dictated he select a wife—and with no further tarrying.

Thus it was no mean satisfaction he gleaned in realising his search had come to an end. Indeed, he couldn't have found a maiden more perfect had he drawn up a list of what he did and did not desire in his countess. He twirled her about the dance floor, his gaze fixed on her countenance.

Her eyes were remarkably fine, more green than hazel, and fringed with long, dusky lashes which emphasised their wideness to a nicety. Her other features were all that was pleasing: a small, neatly shaped nose, and high cheekbones softly tinged with rose; a sensitive mouth, skin clear and silky smooth, and rich dark hair which shone with a healthy lustre, the modish coiffure showing her slender neck to advantage. Certainly a diamond—dashed fine figure, too: slender, though never frail, with a promise of womanly curves beneath her modest white gown.

Her manners, too, were comely: demure, quiet, composed. A lady, to be sure, and a fitting chatelaine for his vast holdings. Her birth was highly respectable, and if her dowry was not, the latter mattered little to one possessed of his great wealth. He envisaged her wearing the coronet of his countess, and found he liked the notion rather well.

The recipient of his concentrated stare shifted in apparent discomfort, bringing Nicolas to an awareness of his open regard. She lost her timing, and though he escaped the ultimate embarrassment of treading on her toe, his hand tightened on her slim waist. He held her a tad closer than necessary, righting their waltzing steps with consummate skill. He forced a smile, mentally labelling himself an ogling dolt. Nevertheless, he managed a smooth apology, explaining his rudeness with the soft words, "You're very lovely."

Heat suffused her cheeks, and her eyes widened a fraction, though not with the girlish delight one might expect from a debutante who had received a pretty compliment from a wealthy peer of the realm. She managed not to miss another step and to lift her lips in the semblance of a smile, but in truth, Miss Claire Dempsey was in an agony of distress.

If there was one man in the whole of London, nay England, whose attention she had hoped not to attract, it was Nicolas Shea, Earl of Kenton. He was wealthy, titled, eligible . . . and in search of a wife; Claire found none of these attributes appealing. Worse, he was coldly handsome, formidable to a fault and displayed an attitude of such self-possession as to make her shiver. Should he offer, she feared she might not be able to refuse.

Though her serene countenance remained unmarred, she was prey to a great deal of unholy resentment. Drat the Marriage Mart, and in particular, this most holy of holies, Almack's. Drat her mother's glee upon at last receiving the coveted vouchers. And drat the Earl of Kenton. He put her nerves all about. Dread had gnawed at her insides the moment he entered the room tonight, making straight for Lady Jersey. Her mother had gushed with pleasure when that lady presented him to her daughter, thereby giving them her permission to waltz. Her father, too, had beamed with unconcealed approval as they made their way to the dance floor.

Oh, rue the day she was born, the eldest of three daughters who must needs marry well so that her sisters might also enjoy the honour of being presented to Society and her brother might have the best education money could buy. Blast the fact they were so damnably poor that all their hopes must be placed on her beauty and ability to bring a suitable parti up to scratch.

But not the Earl of Kenton! she pleaded silently. Would that she had the courage to snub him. But the remembrance of the hope her parents placed in her was not to be rejected. Indeed, they had scraped together all their meagre resources, staking them on the one chance that their beautiful daughter would snare just such a man as the earl.

It mattered not at all that her heart was given to another, especially to someone who followed the drum and had but a modest income. What if he *were* the most handsome man in all of England, with the most irresistible charm? Indeed, he cast the earl's suave, distinguished looks quite into the shade! But he was neither titled nor wealthy, and the only life he could offer was that of a soldier's wife.

Her fervent prayer had been that she would fail to receive a more eligible offer—which was precisely why she had studiously avoided his lordship during her weeks in Town. Still, she had experienced his unwavering gaze upon her more than once, the same gaze she had so recently endured, and it never failed to send tremors of alarm along her spine. She'd even dreamed of slate-grey eyes measuring her, always cold and calculating.

"Do you enjoy life in the country, Miss Dempsey?"

His quiet, cultured tones jolted her back to the present. For a moment, she stared blankly at the perfection of his cravat, a small portion of her brain recognising the Mathematical. She was conscious of his hand at her waist, searing her skin through her satin gown, and of the latent strength of his arms as he twirled her about.

"Oh, yes indeed," she rushed to reply. "I must say I find London most entertaining; however, I do believe I'm far more suited to country life." She shut her mouth then, not wanting to appear as nervous as she was.

"Mmm," he agreed. "I too prefer the life of the country gentleman as opposed to the Town Buck."

Oh, famous, she thought, though her lips lifted in a pretty smile. "And what passes your time in the country, my lord?" she felt the need to enquire, though she hesitated to show any interest.

"Dealing with my estates, mainly, though I do pursue other interests." An unsatisfactory answer, but it seemed he had no wish to elaborate. "Tell me about your family."

It was more an order than a request, but her courtesy and upbringing demanded she comply. If anger flashed in her eyes, she hastily subdued it. While staring dutifully at the folds of his starched cravat, she gratified him with information of her three sisters, all waiting to make their debuts within the next few years, and of her younger brother, who was down from Eton for summer vacation.

"And are all these young ones still at home in . . . is it Sussex?"

How had he known they resided in Sussex? How much more did this man with the cold grey eyes know about her? Claire found her voice, albeit weakly. "Yes, my lord, and no, they are all in London at present. You may find it strange, but my parents have taken an active role in the upbringing of their children, going so far as to insist we all come together at dinner. Unless, of course, we're entertaining a large number of guests."

"Commendable of them, I'm sure," he commented in the calm, cultured tones which emphasised his air of self-possession. "I should like very much to do the same with my own children. It is my hope to find a wife with the same views as mine."

Alarm flared and her eyes widened. She rapidly lowered her lashes, hoping it looked an act of modesty rather than concealment. The last bars of the music struck, and refusing a sigh of relief, she summoned every ounce of composure whilst her escort returned her to her parents.

As expected, her mother was beside herself at the honour paid her daughter. Claire dared not glance at her father lest he see the dismay writ in her eyes. His lordship favoured her with a stately bow, requested a second dance for later in the evening, and almost succeeded in undoing her calm facade. She could but smile and nod, what with her mother near crowing with delight and her father rubbing his hands with pleasure.

No sooner had he moved away, his spine straight, his gait smooth and graceful, than Lady Dempsey turned to Claire with ill-concealed excitement.

"My lovely angel!" she gushed. "To think! The Earl of Kenton! Two dances! Securing approval for the *waltz!* What an honour—so generous, so kind!"

So rich, thought Claire despairingly. Drat the Earl of Kenton's icy eyes! He walked to the card room, making the fact that he'd singled her out more noticeable. After weeks of watching her from the sidelines and requesting a minimum of quadrilles since their first introduction, he was now signalling his intentions. She must discourage him!

"Well done, daughter." Sir Percival's gentle hand rested for a moment on her shoulder, squeezing slightly before falling back to his side. "The Catch of the Season…look, already you have envious mamas casting you acid glances. I'd say we're in a fair way to seeing our dreams fulfilled."

"Surely it's too soon to hope, Papa?" she choked out, casting a furtive gaze about the room. She scarce noticed the misses and their mamas twittering behind their fans, casting hostile glances in her direction. She searched instead for a face she knew she wouldn't find; a mere Major Robert West couldn't hope to procure a voucher to Almack's. If only she could show her parents this night—indeed, this moment—where her heart truly lay.

She couldn't marry the earl—not when her affections, her love, were given to her major. He set her heart aflutter with his caressing blue eyes and flirtatious grin. Some might call him immature and reckless, but she couldn't consider such things slanderous. Indeed, they were part of his charm, making him romantic, dashing and full of life. Why, he had confessed his heart was captured by his green-eyed witch, and he was all she desired in a husband.

"I'm sure it is not too soon." Her father's words washed over her head as she gloomily contemplated the toes of her slippers. "To think," murmured Sir Percival, satisfaction and hope lacing his tone, "that my daughter would snare the most eligible bachelor of the Season. 'Tis truly an answered prayer!"

An answer to *whose* prayer? Claire wondered, holding her chin at a proud angle lest it dare to tremble. The beginning of the quadrille, her second dance with the earl, brought them back together. She did all which was proper, lifting her lips in what she hoped would be construed as a shy smile in answer to the warm one he bestowed upon her. Her parents looked on; she must behave, must pretend—pretend she welcomed the attentions of this man, pretend she was enjoying this interminable dance, this eternal night.

The eyes of the haut ton were fixed upon her, boring into her back, censuring her every move. Earlier, she'd even heard one turbaned dowager explaining in overloud tones that the reason they'd received vouchers was due to "a person of consequence" speaking privately to a lady patroness on their behalf. Some young miss had twittered that it must have been the earl himself, which statement earned a sharp rebuke from her mama. But the frosty dowager had merely inclined her head. Claire had denied herself the sought-after glass of orgeat, and escaped, only thankful her mama hadn't heard such slander.

It was, however, one more black mark against the lofty Earl of Kenton. She fit her steps to his, deciding she hated him: hated him for noticing her, for dancing with her, for singling her out from among the bevy of beauties the Season had to offer. She hated the intent she saw writ in his eyes, the look of interest and purpose.

The anger and frustration of the matchmaking mamas could in no way equal her own. Her plan of escaping his attention had been thwarted, and she wanted to scream at the injustice of it. She felt like the perfect pawn, and wondered if she dared place the blame of her predicament at God's feet. After all, it was He who had created her the eldest of five children, making her beautiful and poor; He who had created the Earl of Kenton, giving him a lithe, supple physique, a suave handsomeness and wealth. And He who had created Major Robert West, the man who could, and had, stolen her heart. It just wasn't fair.

Far and above these considerations, however, was the fear of the choice she might be required to make. She placed her hand lightly on his lordship's arm, allowing him to return her to her parents. As she sank into a curtsy, her gaze lifted to the diamond winking from his cravat, and then to his face, a face made all the more frightening by the warm interest she detected there. He lifted her gloved fingers to his lips, the moist heat of his breath filtering through the thin fabric. She watched him depart, a shiver creeping along her spine. Would she honour her duty, or would she honour her heart? She sent a prayer heavenward in hopes she wouldn't be required to make that decision.

CLAIRE STOOD at her bedchamber window. A shiny black curricle drawn by two high-stepping bays carried the Earl of Kenton away from the modest town house her parents had rented for the Season. She felt as if turned to stone; only her hands, spasmodically clutching the folds of her gown, gave evidence of her inner turmoil. The past three days she had merely existed, suffering a tangible sense of impending doom. Her major had been sent out of Town on an errand for the Crown, and his lordship had called each day, sending a costly bouquet the morning following their dances at Almack's.

Truly, she had tried to discourage him. Deciding his lofty lordship would prefer a bride who gushed and fawned over him, she became just the opposite, polite yet reserved, insofar as her mother's eagle eye would permit. Having scarce spoken three sentences for his lordship's ears alone, and judging by the puzzled frowns she'd intercepted, she had imagined success was imminent.

A playful jab in Claire's side brought her wooden glance swinging round to confront her sister Katie, nearly eighteen and the next to be launched. Katie threw her the mischievous glance of a maiden just entering the world of men, and tossed her head, sending a cascade of dark ringlets about her pretty face. "Darling," she said with a smile, "I think I shall call you the countess. That has a nice ring, doesn't it?"

Claire blanched, turning away with a rapid jerk. Escape seeming of paramount importance, her feet automatically took her to the door. Her fingers latched on the knob. In a second she was through the door, making for the stairs, the front portal and fresh air. She wished it were a bad dream, the product of an overwrought imagination. But even as she reached for a discarded bonnet lying atop a table in the hallway, she knew the nightmare was, in fact, reality. The Earl of Kenton had requested a private audience with her father.

"Claire, my dear," called Sir Percival from behind her, "I would see you in the library, if you please."

"Yes, Papa." Her heart fell. Defeated, she turned obedient, if hesitant, steps in that direction. He shut the door behind her with a quiet click. She glanced at him, noting his aura of suppressed excitement. Her shoulders sagged, and had she not captured her bottom lip between her teeth, it surely would have trembled. Sinking onto a chair, she drew a deep breath, folded prim hands in her lap, and returned her father's gaze with a steadiness she was far from feeling.

Beaming with unconcealed satisfaction, he took a seat behind his desk. After clearing his throat, he made his announcement: "God has seen fit to favour us, daughter. The Earl of Kenton, Nicolas Shea, has offered for you." His glee slipped its reins, and he threw back his head and laughed.

Not by the flicker of a lash did Claire betray her dismay. "And?" she prompted in a quiet voice.

His laughter dissolved. His blue gaze flicked sharply over her. "And? Why, I have accepted his suit, of course. Did you think I would do otherwise?"

"I'm not sure I should like to marry him," she offered in a tiny voice, lowering her head.

His expression was the epitome of horror. Gaping at her, he clapped a hand to his brow. "My daughter has run mad!" he wailed. "Think, gel, *think!* The *Earl of Kenton!* A prize worth the capturing! Rich as Croesus, young and handsome. Daughter, I am convinced you are bamming me. You shall be a countess, mistress of many fine homes. You shall never know the insecurity which comes with the lack of gold.

"He's offered a handsome settlement—more generous than I dared to dream. Your sisters will have their come-outs, young Percy his education. God has provided the answer to our every prayer...*and you don't want to marry him?*"

Claire knew everything he said was true. The earl was a regular paragon of virtue, and many a young lady would envy the honour bestowed upon her. They, too, would consider her mad. Her mother, her sisters, her brother—none of them would understand the ordeal she suffered each time Kenton's cool, grey gaze appraised her like a horse at auction. Did she have the breeding? Were her teeth straight enough? Could she produce an heir? Would she grace his home with beauty and dignity?

How could she marry that cold creature! A man who had never once trespassed the bounds of propriety by even *subtly* flirting with her? He watched her every move, as if checking them against his list of requirements for the wife of his exalted person. Robert West loved her as she was... and he said such pretty things!

"I scarce know him, Papa," she said into the silence.

"You shall have the remainder of your life to get to know him." Sir Percival emitted a disgruntled snort. "We know enough *about* him to be sure he's a decent sort of fellow. Sturdy, honest, generous. You know I should never give you to a man whom I considered unworthy. Had I the slightest cause to doubt his integrity, be assured I would have refused him. I have found nothing to fault. He won't beat you, if that's what you fear."

"No, no," she rushed to assure him. "But, well... 'tis simply that I thought I might remain unwed for yet a while—" she grasped at straws "—I am rather young, and... he seems old to me, Papa."

He swatted away her flimsy excuse with a wave of his hand. "Fiddlesticks and nonsense! You're nineteen, past the age when many young women marry. And he's but a lad—scarcely eight-and-twenty. What's that? Eight, nine years? Why, there's ten separating your mama and I, and we have rubbed on quite famously." His sigh was long and heavy. "Daughter, he's taken his time in selecting a wife. You should be honoured he's chosen you. Shows the man has right good sense, if you ask me.''

Shows the man is awfully choosey, if you ask me, Claire thought in silent rebellion. How could she live up to his expectations? And her poor, dear major. How could she bear the thought of life without him? For his sake, and for hers, she had to try just once more.

"I thought perhaps...well...Major West seems rather taken with me," she said in a near whisper.

"Major West." The name fell flat and empty from Sir Percival's tongue. "He's immature and reckless. He'd lead you a merry dance and leave you a poor widow. He hasn't a groat to secure your future. I would never consign a daughter of mine to such a fate."

"Yes, Papa," she murmured. Oh, how Robert's character was defamed, and he had shown her nothing but kindness! Even Papa couldn't countenance him as husband material. It was so unfair! Robert could never hope to compete with the earl, not in breeding or wealth. And she...she would be a sacrificial lamb.

A tapping sounded at the door. Her mother, her face wreathed in smiles, hurried forward and embraced Claire. "Your father's told you the wonderful news?" she cried, surreptitiously wiping a tear from her eye. "We are so overjoyed, my love, so happy for you. Such a feather in your cap!" She stood back, clapping her hands. "So pleased, I know you will be most happy, such a fine young man."

Her sigh of pure pleasure was cut short by her husband's grunt.

"She doesn't want to marry him." His statement was blunt and pointed.

Her mouth dropped open. "Doesn't want to...whyever not?"

"He's too old, she's too young, doesn't know him well enough—"

"Don't be silly, Husband." Falling to her knees at Claire's feet, Lady Dempsey took up her daughter's hands, her face softening. "Oh, I do wish you were more sensible," she said to her spouse. "'Tis only natural bridal jitters. Why, when my papa informed me of your offer, I was quite beside myself for fear of certain marital duties!"

Sir Percival wiped at his receding hairline with a large, serviceable handkerchief. He coughed, a discreet sound in the sudden quiet of the room. "Thought there must be some reason she wasn't swooning with delight."

Lady Dempsey, scarcely hearing him, gazed earnestly into her daughter's face, a face Claire made sure had paled alarmingly. She hadn't yet considered those marital duties. "My darling, 'tis no great hardship, I assure you! But we shan't pursue that topic just now. I realise you must have time to accustom yourself to becoming a bride. But know that God never meant it to be a wretched experience, and indeed, it is not. Why—"

"I thought you weren't going to pursue it?" said Sir Percival.

"Yes, of course, but husband, I pray you will show some sensitivity to the feelings of a maiden."

Claire's heart lodged in the toes of her slippers. All her excuses were being swept away and tidily disposed of. It would never work. They were so pleased, so delighted... and their financial worries would be over. Could she be so selfish as to turn away their hopes and dreams? She was caught, trapped, as sure as a moth in a sticky spider's web.

Sir Percival cleared his throat. "I have invited his lordship to dine with us on the morrow. I need an answer as to whether he can approach you without fear of rejection."

Claire's eyes lifted from the study of her toes. Her gaze tangled with her father's, reading his hopefully expectant enquiry. Her mother's face registered the same eagerness. Her gaze returned to her folded hands, now clasped in a death grip. Should she refuse, they would return to the country, all hopes of a bright and secure future dashed as surely as a frigate against the cliffs of Dover. Should she agree, all her dreams of being held in a loving embrace could be consigned to the devil. The utter silence of the library was dispelled by the muted sound of running feet in the hallway beyond. Percy's muffled laughter penetrated the heavy atmosphere, as did Delight's scream of wrath moments later.

Claire blinked back her tears and, drawing a breath, forced the words past the lump in her throat. "Yes, Papa. You may tell him I will accept his addresses."

CHAPTER TWO

ANOTHER CRUMPLED WAD of paper hit the grate with force. Small flames licked at its outer edges, then devoured it. With a grim stare, Claire watched the scented sheet disintegrate into ashes. Flicking away an angry tear, she resolutely set her quill to a fresh page.

"My dear major," she began again, dismayed to note her tears weren't inclined to abandon her. Rummaging for a handkerchief, she dabbed her eyes. It wouldn't do for her tears to spoil the ink of what she hoped would be her final attempt to inform Robert West of her imminent betrothal.

Dipping the quill in the inkwell, she glanced about the sparsely furnished sitting-room adjoining her bedchamber, hoping to find inspiration in the yellow patterned wallpaper. With a heavy sigh, she wrote, "I should dislike it if you were to learn this from another source, and indeed, I sincerely regret such news must be imparted. However, this very evening, I shall plight my troth to Nicolas Shea, Earl of Kenton." Setting aside the quill, she snatched up the handkerchief and allowed her tears full rein.

What else could she have possibly done? She really hadn't a choice, not from the time her parents had requested an audience in the sitting-room of their country home before their departure for London. That meeting had exuded an air of solemnity, tinged with desperation,

yet laced with a faint trace of hope. Their financial
straits, as well as their plans for her future and theirs, had
been made fully clear. None of them had suspected she
might fall in love with an ineligible *parti*.

No stranger to duty, from the time she could remember Claire had been versed in those accomplishments expected of a genteel maiden, in the proper conduct and
aspirations of the debutante. A Society miss was expected to marry well, for wealth and not for love. She
never suspected she'd follow another path, especially after speaking that evening with her parents. Indeed, she
had dreamed of making that excellent match...except
always, lining these puffy clouds of imagination, was
romance and love. She'd found them all, she realised with
a twist of bitter amusement, though not in the same man.
She could have wealth with one, or she could have romance and love with the other.

Had she a choice, it would be her major. But she had
none. Therefore, the Earl of Kenton would be her lifelong mate. She could scarce bear the thought, but was
resigned to the sacrifice she must make. Her family depended solely upon her actions, and if her own future
looked bleak, then so it must be.

Still, she owed it to Robert, and indeed, to her own
heart, to make this announcement as painless as possible. She reached for the quill, longing to vow her eternal
love and devotion. However, respect for the commitment she was about to make stilled her hand. Instead she
wrote, "I wish you only the best." Signing her name, she
folded the missive, sealed it and went in search of the
footman James, who was discreet enough to see it delivered at once with none the wiser.

Her mission successfully completed, Claire returned to
her room by way of the back stairs, avoiding everyone

save an upstairs maid. Sprawling atop her bed, she stared with unseeing eyes at the frescoed ceiling. She longed to put every memory she had of Robert West in a locket and wear it close to her heart forever. She recalled their first meeting at Lady Somerset's musicale. A tiny smile fleetingly crossed her lips. The daughter of the house had been persuaded to sing—only to acquit herself most awfully—and later, Robert, after being introduced, said for Claire's ears alone, "I make no doubt you can sing like an angel, though 'tis questionable whether you'd be heard, so captivated would everyone be by your beauty."

She closed her eyes, remembering his smile, the caress in his throaty voice and the softness of his chuckle when she blushed. After that, he'd been at almost every function she attended, always the first to sign her dance card, and always ready with a pretty compliment and an engaging grin. How easy he was to laugh with, and how charming were his ways! His presence had made it easier to ignore the Earl of Kenton's silent study of her person, and to also avoid his company.

However, she still hadn't been saved from the ultimate course she must take. The Earl of Kenton was determined, if nothing else. It angered her that Robert West should put forth his best to win her heart, and yet his lordship, with only a modicum of effort, would claim her hand. With a muffled oath, Claire rolled off the bed, kicking a stray slipper across the room. It just was not fair!

Crossing to the wardrobe, she yanked back the door, belligerently scowling at her limited number of suitable gowns. Out of spite, she reached for a drab grey that had come with her from Sussex. Imagining his lordship's reaction, she smiled. A touch of white powder . . . her hair pulled back in a severe knot? Did she dare?

Her lips twitched, and she gave an infinitesimal nod of her head. She would, and hang that dratted Earl of Kenton's stamp of approval! She donned the gown and sat at the vanity. Scraping heavy lengths of hair away from her face, she pulled it into a tight knot and pinned it in a haphazard fashion. The minutes ticked past in rapid succession, each bringing her ever nearer to the time when his lordship would go down on bended knee to ask *that* question.

At least, it was proper that he go down on bended knee; however, Claire fervently hoped he would not. She couldn't bear it if he spewed lies of how she had captured his heart. She wanted no pretty speeches, no vows of undying devotion. Picturing his lordship doing just so, she reached for the powder pot and sniffed. No, she needn't worry that he would behave any way other than exactly as he felt. She suspected he wasn't a man who did what others expected of him, but rather followed a path of being true to himself.

A discreet tap at her door broke through her musings. The powder pot clattered onto the vanity, and Claire scrambled away, scanning the room for a place to hide. Egad, pray it wasn't her mother, for she would surely swoon! All her bold schemes of shocking the earl evaporated in an instant. She slipped behind the curtains at the window just as the door opened.

Katie called her name. Though she didn't reveal her hiding place, Claire relaxed, blowing out her pent breath in a silent sigh. The door closed, and Katie's voice came again. "Claire, I know you're in here. Do come out from behind those curtains."

"Katie," Claire responded testily, "has it ever occurred to you to wait until you're invited before barging into my chamber?'' She stepped from behind the curtains and regarded her sister with a mighty frown.

Katie fell back against the door with a hand to her heart. "Heaven have mercy! Claire Elizabeth Dempsey! Never suppose I shall allow you to present yourself in the drawing-room in such shocking style! Why, Mama would have a fit of the vapours, and Papa would be mortified. And his lordship—whatever would he think?"

"Oh, do hush, Katie, and find something suitable for me to wear!" snapped Claire, already pouring water into the washbasin to scrub her face. "I vow you are the most priggish of sisters. Why, I was only experimenting." And when Katie cast her a dour glance, she snipped, "For my wedding night!"

Katie giggled. "Oh, Claire, never say so! Why, you look prepared for a death march to the guillotine. You're about to accept the proposal of one of the finest men in England, and I own I cannot understand your reluctance to marry him. I vow he's the most handsome of men—I daresay you haven't even noticed how dark his hair is, and how it curls so nicely at his nape. Have you taken note, dear sister, of his legs? I make no doubt he has no need of false calves. And the width of his shoulders—"

"Katie!" Claire admonished. "I'm shocked that you'd inspect my intended so thoroughly! Besides, it isn't proper for young ladies to take note of such things!"

"Oh, pooh. Now who's being the prig? Why, wasn't it but a week ago you were extolling the virtues of one Major West to me? 'Oh, what a fine figure he cuts in his regimentals. Did you see, Katie, how his eyes positively dance?'" Katie quoted. "Why, he flirted with you in the most outrageous fashion the entire time we were at Hatchard's! I can only be thankful Mama and the twins weren't present to witness your behaviour. Now, I believe this lemon satin will be perfect, don't you? It does show your colouring to advantage."

Claire's mouth turned down in a mulish frown. "I don't want to be shown to advantage," she grumped.

"Yes, I know, dearest, but you are expected to do the pretty. Poor Mama is in such whoops that you've actually caught an earl, but your moping is quite near to spoiling her fun. Mind your manners, Claire, for her sake. She and Papa are so delighted, thinking this the greatest of good fortune. They would be overset should they feel they've consigned you to a life of unhappiness."

Sighing, she knelt before Claire, taking up both her hands. "I've been a featherbrain, sis. I thought you merely whiling away the time with Major West, but I saw your face turn so sad when I mentioned him just now. You love him, don't you?"

Claire bowed her head, no proof against this face of sympathy. She nodded. "He's fun and alive, and he sees more than my beauty. However, Papa thinks him immature and reckless. He's obviously poor, while his lordship is rich . . . and we need his money."

Katie's face was eloquent with empathy, her eyes reflecting her helplessness. "I'd marry him for you if I could, dear, truly I would."

Claire's lips lifted in a brief smile. "I know you would. You've always been generous to a fault. The best of good sisters. But, I suppose I must face my fate with a smile. Now do help me dress. Mama will expect my presence in the drawing-room before dinner is announced."

Katie nodded, coming to her feet, and smoothing down her skirts. "Indeed. And Claire, dear, I do pray you'll find happiness with his lordship."

Claire shrugged, holding in check a rampage of emotion. "Oh, I daresay I shall find him tolerable enough."

Her sister cast her a sceptical glance, but said nothing. Minutes later the lemon satin swirled about Claire's ankles. Katie urged her to sit so she might make her coiffure presentable. She laughed as she removed the haphazard array of pins. "I do hope his lordship appoints you an abigail post-haste. Mama should have hired that hairdresser who fixed you up the night you went to Almack's. He turned you out in fine style. I, however, insist you comb these tangles out yourself, and in the meantime, I'll see to whoever is doing all that confounded scratching at your door."

Claire applied the brush to her hair, wincing at the mess she'd made. From behind her, she heard Katie say, "Oh, it's you, James. What is it?" After a pause in which the footman mumbled softly, Katie said, "James, I'm perfectly capable of carrying your missive to her myself. She's right here, but she's busy. Now do hand it over."

Claire swivelled her chair round and stood, curious as to what the footman's seemingly all-important mission was. Moving to the door, she snatched the sealed envelope from Katie's hand just as quickly as that miss had snatched it from James's.

"Thank you, James," she said, turning on her heel, leaving Katie to close the door. Her heart pounded and her fingers trembled. Sitting down at the vanity, she pulled a tallow candle closer, and spread the single sheet before her.

"My green-eyed witch," she read.

Your recent communication has left me distraught and desolate. If we must say our goodbyes, I would they weren't said through cold, formal notes. I be-

seech you to meet me at the entrance to Hyde Park
at midnight tonight. I'll follow you there, seeing you
come to no harm, but don't acknowledge my presence until we're safely away. I beg you to meet me in
this.

Robert.

Claire's gaze fixed on his scrawled signature, the
enormity of his request penetrating her consciousness.
Midnight at Hyde Park? She wasn't sure he knew what
he was asking.

"My green-eyed witch?" murmured Katie from behind her, a suggestion of laughter in her voice.

Claire snatched up the note, clasping it to her bosom.
"Katie! 'Tis none of your business, and don't poke fun!
Haven't you learned not to eavesdrop? You did read it,
didn't you?"

"You can't go, you know," said Katie matter-of-factly.
She retrieved the brush. "Turn round so I can finish your
hair."

"And just why can I not?" demanded Claire, directing a fierce frown through the mirror at her nosy sibling.

"There are any number of reasons why not," Katie
replied, gathering the tresses to create a topknot. "Midnight at Hyde Park? Surely you see the impropriety of it?
You can't go alone, and you dare not take a maid into
your confidence. You will be affianced to the earl, and a
lovers' tryst with Robert West is not at all the thing. I
wonder he should even ask such a thing of you! Papa is
correct in thinking him reckless and immature. It's obvious he's careless of your reputation." She sniffed her
disapproval, and added another pin to Claire's coiffure.

"Oh, Katie, how you prattle!" Claire snapped, deciding against asking for her support. "It's obvious you

know nothing of love. A person in love takes chances—moving mountains if need be. I see nothing wrong with Robert wanting our leavetaking to be more personal, and I'm flattered he cares enough to flout the rules!''

"Bah!" was Katie's sour rejoinder. "You would be forever ruined should you be caught. I think it horrid of him to ask you to place your reputation in such peril, and should I ever see him again, be assured I shall tell him so."

"You wouldn't dare! Oh, beast of all sisters! You would condemn a man for following his heart? How could you?"

Katie's lower lip was set in a determined line. She caught and held Claire's gaze reflected in the glass. "He's asked you to walk through Town in the dead of night, alone but for him. 'Tis not done, and well you know it."

"Of course I know it," Claire said, emitting a sniff of her own. "But you can't blame him for trying, and he never said he *expected* to see me. I daresay he'll understand if I don't appear."

"If?" Katie added the finishing touches to her handiwork by coaxing some wispy tendrils to curl about Claire's face.

"When," corrected Claire. She turned her head this way and that, studying her reflection in the mirror. "Very pretty, Katie. You've surpassed yourself."

"Thank you. Now may I borrow one of your gowns?"

"Certainly." Claire realized Robert's note was still crushed in her fist, and she opened her hand, smoothing the sheet out atop the vanity. Scanning the words once more, she marvelled at how easily she and Robert had fallen in love, and how heartbreakingly short was the time they had enjoyed together. Would those few, now bittersweet, memories be enough to last her through a lifetime? Or did she dare to steal just one more?

"I'd throw that in the fire if I were you," Katie advised from the wardrobe. "I vow it wouldn't be pleasant should someone find it."

"You're always so practical, Katie," Claire returned without rancour. "I shall do just that."

Katie returned her attention to the gowns, and Claire folded the note into a small square, tucking it into the bodice of her lemon satin, next to her heart.

TAKING PORT with a prospective father-in-law, Nicolas decided, wasn't proving the daunting experience he'd feared. Chief among his earlier worries—causing him to discharge his curricle at the gate with the certain knowledge he'd prefer to walk this night's business off—was facing an encroaching toadeater, or worse yet, a father who demanded his little girl be done right by. Sir Percival was, and did, neither. Rather, he indulged in those acceptable topics of hunting and the fox. Nicolas relaxed, much to his surprise.

'Twas scarce a quarter of an hour, however, before Sir Percival rose. "Well, lad, I don't s'pose you'll want to be here 'til the cock crows. Shall we rejoin the ladies?"

Nicolas nodded, a brief smile playing across his mouth. This was it. His first—and, it was to be hoped, last—proposal of marriage was but minutes away. He wondered at the sudden tightening of his stomach muscles, and the sharp little tingle accompanying it. He wasn't nervous. His breath sang a quiet whistle through his teeth as he followed his host to the drawing-room. Seeking a dark-haired, green-eyed beauty, he found her perched on the edge of a sofa, poised as if for flight. He sat beside her, ignoring her nervous little jump.

Claire's gaze was locked on her tightly clenched hands. She didn't look at him, didn't smile. Surely not the most encouraging of signals, Nicolas mused. Dashed uncomfortable, this business. Settling against the back of the sofa, he crossed his booted feet before him. Might as well let the chit become accustomed to his presence before causing her further upset. He accepted a cup of tea from Lady Dempsey with gracious thanks, and inclined his ear towards the pianoforte and Katie, who rendered a rather pretty performance.

Nicolas sipped his tea, deciding dinner had passed tolerably well, if one could accept with equanimity Miss Dempsey's refusal to cast him a glance. Indeed, she'd spared him no more than two, and brief ones at that. She'd been noticeably quiet throughout. However, this fact had doubtless been remarked by no one but him. The other chattering youngsters had more than made up for any lapses in conversation.

The last notes of the music rippled away. Katie moved from the pianoforte, accepting a cup of tea from her mama. Young Percy succeeded in tugging one of the twin's blond curls, and during the ensuing screech, Nicolas grasped his chance.

"Miss Dempsey," he said without preamble, "would you care to accompany me on a stroll about the garden?"

She turned deathly pale, but graciously accepted. Every member of the family came to attention, forgetting pulled hair and chastisements, he noted with some discomfort. Mama and Papa Dempsey smiled benignly. The twins' smirks were positively impish.

"I daresay I should walk with you," said young Percy importantly, puffing out his chest.

"I daresay you should not," returned Papa Dempsey without hesitation.

One of the twins, heaven knew which one, made a light, teasing comment, sending Claire into blushing confusion.

All of them obviously knew just what would transpire in the garden. A damned beastly business, this. Indeed, he had been quite mistaken when he'd reckoned the task would be easy. It certainly hadn't been thus far.

He held open the garden doors. Claire slipped through under the attentive eyes of her family. Nicolas closed the doors quietly behind him, thankful for the dim light and the cool night air. He placed a solicitous hand at the small of Claire's back, guiding her down the two shallow stairs and into the moonlight beyond.

For days, he had rehearsed the words, repeating them over and again in his mind. He thought this mental practice would stand him in good stead, and the proposal would roll off his tongue smooth as honey. But the thing of it was, every time he opened his mouth to speak, the question seemed caught there, refusing utterance.

A dashed nuisance, this business of securing a wife. And what an aloof wife! So proper, so dignified, so... unreceptive. It almost gave him cause to think she didn't much care for the thought of marrying him. Was it possible she might refuse his offer?

His stomach muscles constricted at the thought. Egad, he'd sent a note to the countess yesterday, requesting she remove herself to London with all haste to set preparations in order for his wedding. And he'd already applied for a special licence. *Getting rather ahead of yourself, are you not, Kenton?* he silently admonished himself. *Too cocksure by half.*

But, Nicolas consoled himself, she wouldn't refuse. Her father's reaction had been more than positive, relaying the certain message that his suit was highly acceptable. He hadn't spent years on the Town, being sought after by every grasping mama the ton offered, to remain innocent of his consequence, and what it meant.

'Twas a bitter thought, but one he could most times effectively banish. He'd learned some years ago that he would never be accepted and loved for who he was, but rather for what he had to give. That knowledge led him to choose a wife with extra care, for if he had to buy a wife, he expected a fair deal in return.

And Miss Claire Dempsey was certainly that. Exceedingly fair. He only wished he were confident enough to prolong their courtship, giving them both a chance to further their acquaintance. But such a diamond would be besieged with suitors and offers, and he wasn't about to take the chance that one of those might be more handsome or more desirable than he. Besides, he couldn't outguess Fate or be certain he'd have a full lifetime in which to sire an heir. He was in need of a wife right now and in his estimation, Miss Dempsey was a prime candidate.

He cast a sidelong glance at her. Hands clasped before her, she hadn't once looked his way. What occupied her silent thoughts? Why hadn't she engaged him in inane, mindless chatter? Mayhap she was nervous to be walking with him in the dimly lit garden.

While applauding her modesty and decorum, he still wondered if there was a warm, spontaneous woman beneath her cool facade. It had seemed so, that first night he'd seen her standing across the ballroom, laughing at a comment made by one of her gawky admirers. She seemed a different person now, distant and reserved.

His afternoon calls had been met with a reticent politeness. He was thanked prettily for his bouquet of flowers, but otherwise, the short visits had done little to further their acquaintance. Indeed, she had seemed rather contrary, in a purposeful and quiet way. She had neither encroached nor encouraged, and he had found he rather more enjoyed the company of her family.

The next promising beauty in line, Katie, was practical, yet full of laughter. The twins, Deirdre and Delight, at sixteen, were the epitome of mischief, and not at all concerned about their behaviour before a lord. He liked that. It showed a freedom of spirit he hoped for in his own children, should he be blessed with such. Young Percy, at eleven, was full of pranks, yet a delightful boy for all of that. It only left for Miss Dempsey to acknowledge his presence, and he would feel perfectly well satisfied in his choice of mate.

They had now taken two turns about the tiny garden without so much as a cough issued between them. He glanced at Claire's lovely face. Her fine green eyes stared expressionlessly straight ahead. Botheration! They were as well as engaged. Why must he speak the words? 'Twas a mere formality...and a nasty business which must needs be done.

"May we sit?" He indicated a small bench nestled between two rosebushes. Reading the small inclination of her head as agreement, he drew her down beside him. Pulling in a deep, rose-scented breath, he forced the reluctant words off his tongue.

"Miss Dempsey, I would be honoured if you will be my wife." He groaned inwardly, closing his eyes for a brief second. That didn't sound in the least as he had planned. 'Twas no question at all! Surely he could have employed a tad more finesse, he thought with derision. What a dashed looby he'd become. He might have even thrown himself to his knees before her.

He discarded the notion instantly, certain that she would deplore such an act of devotion as much as he. He tried once more. "Will you be my wife?" he asked softly.

Claire's lashes dropped of their own volition, and she drew in air between her teeth. Straightening her shoulders and lifting her head, she looked him directly in the eyes. "My lord," she said, her words steady, though quiet, "I am perplexed as to why you should have chosen me when I've offered you no encouragement. Do you not desire even a modicum of affection from your spouse?"

Twin black brows rose and fell in rapid succession. One corner of his finely etched mouth turned up in wry derision. "No, Miss Dempsey, I do not," he said, his cultured tones soft yet firm. "It's been my experience that false affection is more destructive than no affection at all. I would have neither of us feel it necessary to perpetrate a lie. I rather think people deal more honestly with one another when nothing of that sort is expected of them."

He took her hand in both of his, playing with her fingers in an abstracted manner. "Miss Dempsey, I've chosen you because you possess several qualities I admire. I feel it possible we might deal tolerably well together."

She didn't flinch as his cool grey gaze appraised her face, searching her eyes in the gloom. Indeed, she held his look, delving as deeply into his eyes as he did hers, until some infinitesimal emotion—fear? certainly not attraction!—stirred within. She lowered her lashes and whispered, "Then I've been selected simply because I've been found acceptable?"

The realisation of her worst fears was difficult to own. He truly *was* cold and bloodless. Robert's note tickled her breast, a constant and forceful reminder of the man who loved her for who she was. She concentrated on his lordship's hands, which still idly caressed her fingers, noticing for the first time the long and slender strength of them.

"I should not have offered for you had I found you unacceptable," came his enigmatic acknowledgement. "I'm aware we haven't had much time to come to know each other. I'm also certain there are many adjustments to be made in a marriage. I will endeavour to accustom myself to your character, and I hope I may expect the same from you. If, that is, you agree to be my wife."

Claire stared across the garden, feeling a certain sadness, a wistfulness or melancholy which threatened to cause her lower lip to tremble. Silently, she bade goodbye to all her hopes for the future. Goodbye to loving arms. Goodbye to laughing blue eyes. She turned to him, with her head held high. "Yes, my lord," she murmured. "I will be your wife."

He lifted her hand, his lips scarcely grazing her fingertips. "You've made me a happy man, Miss Dempsey."

And you, my lord, she thought with burning resentment, *have made me the most wretched of all women.*

CHAPTER THREE

NICOLAS FELT like a new man. Certainly one having discharged the last of his burdens, and pleased at having made an excellent business venture. He strode down the stairs at the main entrance of Sir Percival's home, glad he'd elected to walk off this night's task.

While having to propose and await acceptance was onerous, the past two hours spent in the library with his future father-in-law were pleasurable. Drinking fine brandy, a treat he suspected was purchased for just such an occasion, they'd drawn up preliminary settlements to the mutual satisfaction of both parties. Sir Percival had agreed without hesitation to the special licence, not knowing it had already been applied for. The sooner he could return to the country, he'd said, the happier he'd be. And they needn't wait for a wedding gown as Claire would wear the one her mother and grandmother had married in.

Nicolas's quiet sigh was relieved and happy. All was in order and running smoothly. A few more necessary arrangements, and all that would be left was to say "I do." He felt remarkably lighthearted and free of worry.

Extending a hand to throw back the latch of the wrought-iron gate, he caught a slight movement from the corner of his eye. His gloved fingers stilled on the cool metal. Peering through the dark night, lit only marginally by the sparse street lamps, he saw the slender figure of a woman, slipping furtively from the mews behind his host's house. She was draped from head to toe in a dark cloak, the hood pulled tightly about her head, shrouding her face. A maid, no doubt, and judging by her secretive manner, stealing the household silver. Waiting but a moment, he quietly lifted the latch to follow her.

The hooded figure hurried past the row of darkened houses and another figure disengaged itself from the shadows, following her at a short distance. *More and more intriguing,* thought Nicolas, setting off in silent pursuit. A nattily dressed young man, one certainly not of the serving orders, dogging the heels of a housemaid? What mischief was afoot?

Years of practising the art of stealth stood Nicolas in good stead. The man and the maid, oblivious of his presence, slipped inside the gates of Hyde Park with him but a moment behind. He crouched beside a manicured hedge, glad of his sombre attire and the nearby street lamp's weak illumination bypassing his nook. The maid cast herself into the man's arms. Her hood fell back, feeble fingers of light caressing her face.

Nicolas nearly gasped with incredulity. Claire! His betrothed! Slipping away for an assignation with her lover! Shock rooted him to the spot, preventing him from confronting the illicit pair.

"Oh, Robert," sighed Claire, "I was so afraid it wasn't you behind me. I feared I would turn to find a bogeyman!"

Robert West chuckled, squeezing her tightly. "Of course it was me. I assured you I'd be right behind you." He combed his fingers through her unbound hair. "Claire, darling…relieve my heart and say it's a lie!" he said with hushed emotion. "Tell me you haven't pledged yourself to another!"

Claire's nerves were at razor's edge. Betrothed barely hours before, she couldn't accept with equanimity the impropriety of coming here. She allowed her major to hold her a moment longer, then gently eased away.

"You shouldn't have asked me to come, Robert. It's highly improper, so I mustn't stay. I've come only to say goodbye...and to tell you I shall never forget you." Only the ragged sigh escaping her lips gave evidence of her inner heartbreak.

"Claire..." Her name fell, featherlight, from his lips. "You mustn't marry him. Marry me! Come with me tonight. We shall elope to Gretna Green. If your betrothal hasn't yet been announced, no one save your family will be the wiser. Say you'll come with me now."

His voice pleaded urgently, and for an instant, as she beheld the fevered light in his eyes, Claire came near to accepting. She wanted nothing more than to return to his arms, to rest her head against his shoulder, to have him soothe away the agony of duty and her fear of the future with a strong, sun-bronzed hand. But she stepped away, shaking her head.

"Robert, I feel sure you haven't given proper consideration to such a suggestion. I have given my word. And I could never do that to my family, nor to the...to my fiancé."

"Hang them!" expostulated Robert, his blue eyes narrowing with determination. "What about us, Claire? You and I? Do you sell yourself for love or money?"

Her head snapped back as if she'd been slapped. "You've no right to speak such things to me," she said, a betraying quaver trembling in her voice. "I bid you goodbye, Major West."

She made to sweep past him, but he caught her shoulders and pulled her into his arms. "Forgive me, forgive me," he murmured. "I cannot bear the thought of you wedding another."

"It has to be," she said woodenly, her anger melting.

"Why does it have to be? Have you no choice?" He sighed raggedly at the tiny shake of her head. "Ah, Claire, why him?"

His muscles bunched in sudden tension, as if he'd said something he'd regretted. "Why do you say that?" she asked.

"May I kiss you, Claire?"

"Robert, I am betrothed," she protested, at wit's end. What was he about? "I *can't*. And you didn't—"

"You *can!* Who will know?"

"I will! I should hate to live with my conscience."

"Mayhap I should steal one, then." His warm fingers moved beneath her chin, lifting her head, raising her lips to his.

"Not if you value your life, you won't." The voice growled like thunder, threatening from directly behind them.

Startled, Claire ripped herself from the major's arms. West muttered an oath and whirled on his heel.

"I can't say I appreciate you holding my fiancée so closely, Major," Kenton grated savagely. "Will you say goodbye, or must I ask you to secure your seconds?"

Robert stepped back a few paces, regarding his assailant with a wariness tinged with anger. He spared a glance for Claire, and his rigid stance relaxed a small degree. "No need for such measures," he muttered.

"Mayhap it won't come to that, then," agreed Kenton, his voice slashing like a deadly rapier. "I might inform you I have witnessed *all* that has transpired here. I suggest the incident be forgotten. I shan't want to hear of

it again, by any means. . . ." The unspoken threat was
unmistakable.

Robert's eyes glittered in the feeble light of a waning
moon and shadowed lamp. He executed a slight bow to
Claire, and raised her hand, his lips grazing her fingertips. "Goodbye, Claire."

"Goodbye." Her voice was but the merest whisper. He
turned and melted into the Park. She watched, miser-
able.

She stared at the trees behind which he disappeared,
not daring a glance at her betrothed. Never had she felt
so...so *trapped*. She begged God to open the ground and
swallow her up. Chagrin warred with shame, and had she
not cautioned herself to discipline, she might have indulged in a fit of temper. Instead, she summoned her
voice, "How came you to be here, my lord?"

"I was leaving your father's house, having just finished drawing up marriage settlements, when I saw what
I thought was a thieving maid sneak away."

Claire heard the tightly leashed rage in his voice, the
disgust and contempt, and inwardly flinched.

"Tell me, Miss Dempsey," he continued, his tone in-
flexible, "will I be taking a virgin to wife?"

She gasped, her gaze snapping to his face, to his rock-
hard jaw and the icy slits of his eyes. "My lord," she
choked out in a strangled voice, "I have never once even
kissed him!"

"That doesn't precisely answer my question."

She searched his face, hoping to find some softening.
Seeing none, she wondered what she might say to soothe
the hackles of this ruffled beast. "Yes," she stated with
a resigned sigh. Then, lest he misconstrue her answer and
find cause to take umbrage, she felt compelled to add, "I
have not yet known a man."

She was thankful of the dim light, for her face grew
very hot indeed.

"Have you ever conducted an assignation of this nature before?"

She hung her head, her words a whisper in the night.
"No, my lord."

"Come, I shall escort you home."

He offered his arm. After a moment's hesitation, her
fingers touched the fine material of his coat and settled
on the rigid muscles beneath. He was angry, incredibly
so, and she dared not speak a word of either explanation
or apology.

They walked several blocks in a heavy, breath-crushing
silence. She sensed his considerable effort to control his
wrath, while she was busy fighting dismay. Caught red-
handed, with Robert West summarily dismissed from her
life. And his lordship...would he break off their engagement? If he did, she would be ruined, returned in
disgrace to their country seat. Kenton would have to tell
her father why, lest he be sued for breach of contract. She
squeezed her eyes tight, banishing the picture of her parents' dismay at the news of her iniquity. She doubted she
would be able to bear looking them in the face again.

The streets were eerie, deserted, not a carriage dis-
turbing the calm. For the first time, Claire was glad of his
lordship's presence. He stood quite six feet tall, and she
had little doubt that his lithe physique contained the
promise of raw power. She was even thankful of his supporting arm; her legs were as weak as a newborn colt's.

He came to a sudden halt beneath a street lamp and
faced her. His warm breath blew across her cheek, and
his finger touched her chin, tilting her face upwards. He
studied her for some moments. Her gaze met his in a
searching question, refusing to shy away. His other hand

abstractedly smoothed her hair away from her face. His fingers entwined in the silken strands, until it apparently dawned on him what he was doing. He abruptly dropped his hands, linking them together behind his back.

"You understand," he said slowly, a thread of anger still rippling through his voice, "I question whether I should continue this . . . engagement. 'Tis not a matter to be lightly considered. However, before I commit my energies, I should like to know if you are of a mind to break it."

Claire gulped, but still refused to cower before him. "No, my lord," she said, looking him directly in the eye, "I am not."

"And if I elect to continue, do I have your word that you'll stay faithful to our pledge?" he rasped.

Her gaze locked with his icy grey one. Again that unsettling tremor of emotion, certainly fear, coursed through Claire. She drew a deep breath. "You have my word. I promise."

"Very well. I shall call on you tomorrow afternoon with my decision. Be prepared to go driving—I daresay we'll need some privacy."

NICOLAS TAPPED on the roof of the hired hackney and instructed the driver to let him down. Skirting the light of a street lamp, he passed a generous amount of coin into the old man's hand and sent him on his way. He doubted Lord Renshaw, Castlereagh's underling, would be pleased he was late for their meeting, but dared to hope his superior would be glad to see him, anyway. And that he'd be willing to give Major Robert West his marching orders.

That, thought Nicolas, was of paramount importance. And far more preferable than meeting the man on the Heath—which, in the heat of his anger, was precisely what he'd wanted to do. But no, there were more civilised ways to accomplish his aim. Besides, Miss Dempsey would hardly thank him if he spilled her lover's blood. However, should West choose to talk, he would face him over duelling pistols, and civilised ways be damned.

Reaching Pall Mall, Nicolas spared a glance down the quiet street, noting the stillness of the night before slipping into an alley beyond. Had he not guessed sooner, Miss Dempsey's escapade assured him he was taking an unwilling bride. Rather famous, he thought with a certain cynicism, that he should choose the one miss in all of London who found the idea of marriage to him repugnant. 'Twas a surprising and even unsettling realisation: he was engaged to a woman who wanted neither him nor his money.

Amazing, too, that she should be forced to marry him. His hours with Sir Percival had given him a fair idea of how their finances lay. Now he realised she must feel honourbound to do her duty by her family. Noble of her, but it made him angrier still. Once again his money, not his person, had paved his way. He sighed, slipping silently inside an open gate. What else had he expected? He'd bought a wife . . . not her affection.

An acceptable wife. The words flashed like a lightning bolt through his brain. Acceptable she was not! He wondered if his wits had gone a'begging that he hadn't immediately pronounced an end to their betrothal. Would it were as simple as that, he thought with a wry twist of his lips. And now the knowledge that he came between two lovers made him feel like a worse blackguard. He shook his head with resignation. Padding down the scullery stairs, he tapped a short tattoo on the door.

"Good very early morning to you, Kenton. You look in fine fettle."

Nicolas removed his gaze from the study of his boots, and assessed his host. Lord Benjamin Renshaw had been his superior since he and Andrew Marsh, Viscount Rutledge, had undertaken their first spying mission against Napoleon's forces three years before. Since then, he and Andrew had worked together, ferreting out political dispatches and secret communications. It had been a rather undemanding undertaking... until now.

"My lord," he acknowledged, taking note of Renshaw's brocade dressing-gown and stockingless feet stuffed into soft slippers. "I might say the same of you. I see, however, that you've misplaced your nightcap again."

"Told you I don't wear one," Renshaw responded, softly closing the door. "And you wouldn't find me *en déshabillé* if you arrived at the appointed hour. I was that near to giving up on you." He spoke in hushed tones, leading Nicolas through deserted hallways and into his panelled study.

Nicolas helped himself to a chair whilst his host closed the door. Crossing his booted feet, he leaned back his head and closed his eyes, willing his mind to focus on the business at hand. "Renshaw," he said, his lashes flickering up, "tell me you've had news of Andrew."

"Not as yet." Renshaw shook his head, his brow creased in a frown. "It's been five weeks. I fear he's dead."

Nicolas straightened, rubbing his hand over weary eyes. Andrew's current mission was to seek out a list of names of traitors to the English Crown. Nicolas was the go-between, meeting Andrew in France and taking his news to Renshaw. Renshaw believed the group's ringleader was an English nobleman and was determined to find him. The English nobleman was obviously just as determined he would not. Andrew, Nicolas believed, had found his list . . . and Andrew was missing.

"He can't be dead. Why would they be so hell-bent on killing me if they've silenced him? They wouldn't waste their time unless they feared he'd get his information to me."

"Mayhap," Renshaw admitted with a shrug, handing him a glass of brandy before settling onto the chair opposite him. "Unless they suspect you're already in possession of certain damning facts. The problem, Kenton, is that we don't know what they think. We only know they've found you out. There were—what?—three attempts made on your life while you were in France looking for Andrew. I'd say they were serious about getting rid of you."

This reminder of his mortality did nothing to improve Nicolas's mood. It only served to procure visions of the line of Kenton dying with him and thoughts of Miss Claire Dempsey . . . the woman he'd hoped might circumvent such a disaster. "Which only strengthens my opinion that Andrew is still alive and in possession of the all-important list of names. I think he's found himself a hidy-hole and has our traitors and a whole slew of French soldiers keeping him rooted in it. I was close to him, but I don't know how they found me out."

"One does wonder," Renshaw admitted, cocking a brow.

"I hope you aren't suggesting Andrew was caught, and told all?" was Nicolas's deceptively mild response. "You know as well as I that he was hand-picked for his honour and integrity. Not to mention that as my friend, he would never knowingly hasten my demise." He tilted his head, drained his glass and set it aside.

"I'm suggesting no such thing," Renshaw returned, his manner just as calm. "It could be as you say, that he's gone to ground. Unless, of course, he's dead and they don't know it. But, he never intersected with you, which certainly suggests he was unable to do so.

"It's my guess they figured he'd make for the coast and thought to intercept him there. Finding your boat only confirmed their supposition that they'd lit on your point of rendezvous. It seems we're not dealing with people of intelligence, Kenton. Our English nobleman, whoever he may be, has chosen thugs to do his dirty work.

"Had they an ounce of sense between them, they would have made a slow leak in your boat and you wouldn't have realised it until you were in the middle of the Channel. Instead, what did they do? They smashed the craft. I applaud their thinking abilities. Being the wily fox you are, you slipped out of their hands. The old man you hired to get you back across the Channel wasn't so fortunate. He's been found with his throat neatly slit."

"My wits are obviously dulled," drawled Nicolas, his lips curling in a dry salute. Probably, he acknowledged, because they were consumed with a certain green-eyed beauty whose fate rested in his hands. Her future wouldn't be pretty should he cry off. She would be ruined, returned to the country in utter disgrace, never to outlive the folly of one imprudent action.

Reaching for the brandy decanter, he refilled his glass. "I might have known you were paving the way for just such an announcement. I only wonder you got round to relaying the news so quickly. You must be eager for your bed. When was he found?"

"I received the tidings but hours ago. My informant discovered his body in the bushes, said he'd been dead for some time. I think it safe to surmise that he gave your description, alerting our traitors to your person. Hence the attempts on your life when you returned to find Andrew. My informant also tells me they've asked questions of a certain innkeeper, who, by the by, is still alive."

Renshaw steepled his hands, clicking his tongue. "And there you are. It won't be long before they come up with the Earl of Kenton as their prime target. You're not safe in France, and soon you won't be safe in England, either. I don't know how long we might keep them at bay once they learn your name. Which brings us back to where we started. You need to lie low, resuming your duties as go-between, and I need to appoint a man to find Andrew."

Nicolas sipped his brandy, considering the implications of this information. Andrew had the names of the traitors, but was helpless until he reached English soil. He, Nicolas, though not precisely helpless, didn't know who his enemies were. He needed Andrew's information as soon as may be, for how much longer could he hope to remain anonymous? Long enough to live down a scandal and find a different bride? Dared he take the chance? Looking across to Renshaw, he asked, "I suppose I'll be required to share all my knowledge with the man who replaces me?"

"Naturally. I daresay you'll have to polish him up a bit, which will necessitate your removing to your estate for a few days. He, by the way, is aware of your identity."

"And no doubt you'll make me aware of his in your own sweet time. Whilst you await that perfect moment, I should like to request a favour of you. I would take it most kindly if you will give a certain Major Robert West his marching orders.''

Renshaw always seemed to find the perfect moment to spill his information, while he, Nicolas, never managed that feat. It was left to him to blurt his desires in a way which could never be called sly. But Renshaw's words only strengthened his resolve. If he couldn't be in Town, then so help him, neither would the major. Anyone could see that Miss Dempsey was innocent as a babe, and he didn't want that scoundrel leading her astray.

"Odso! Has he been hanging about the skirts of the fair damsel I hear you're taken with? A rather handsome rapscallion, is he not? Well, I must say I'm inordinately pleased you're already acquainted with him—he is your new cohort."

Renshaw chuckled into the sudden, tense silence. "I never thought to see you put out of countenance, Kenton.''

Nicolas clamped shut his jaw, his black brows snapping together. "He's not the man for the job. Why, he's—'' What was he to say? Loud as a pack of hounds baying after a fox? How could he confess he knew the man possessed no talent for stealth without giving Claire away? "I shouldn't think his conduct and reputation for recklessness would indicate him as the man for this position.''

"His sort of daring is just what we need.''

"You truly think he's capable?'' asked Nicolas through clenched teeth, trying to subdue his own personal enmity. He wanted to slam his fist down onto the arm of his chair, proclaiming in no uncertain terms that he refused to work with the wretch. But Renshaw would want to know why, and even if he should admit to having taken a decided dislike to the man, it wouldn't wash.

"I do. And Castlereagh agrees. Major West happens to be my aforementioned informant, and our only hope."

"Is he aware of his new duties?"

"Not as yet. I'll speak with him later this morning. He'll be instructed to forgo shaving, keep growing his hair and to meet you in Dover tomorrow. I can give him your direction, so you needn't worry about anything but meeting him at your door."

"So kind," murmured Nicolas, rising to his feet. "I bid you good day, Renshaw."

"Mmm," grunted Renshaw. "Oh, and Kenton, all things considered, do you really think it the time to take a wife? Have you thought that it might be dangerous for her?"

One black brow rose at this challenge to his integrity. "I've given the matter careful consideration, my lord, and shall take every care to assure myself of her safety. I wouldn't marry if I feared she'd suffer." And she wouldn't suffer, not if he was killed; at least, he would hardly leave her heartbroken. He lifted his shoulders in a shrug. "I haven't any choice but to take a wife. Should I die without issue, I shall be the last Earl of Kenton."

Minutes later, Nicolas strode through the night, sucking cool air into his lungs. So, he was to play host to a man he would as soon throttle. No doubt West had deduced why Nicolas was taking Claire to wife, and like Renshaw, thought Nicolas was placing her life in jeopardy.

Well, West couldn't offer her anything better. Indeed, his life would soon be placed in the gravest of danger. Supposing, that was, Nicolas should decide to release her from their engagement. But, all things considered, he didn't think that the wisest course of action. Besides, he thought, finally acknowledging the irrational, illogical little idea which kept niggling at him…he didn't want to let her go.

CHAPTER FOUR

THE HOURS until 5:00 p.m., when the earl would arrive to take her driving, wore hard on Claire's nerves. Concern for her immediate future had made for a restless night and an equally agitated day, and now, as she dressed for the drive, she knew a certain relief in that her fate would soon be announced.

Her confidence was shaken, so she dressed with care, choosing a fetching white muslin gown, with tiny red roses embroidered about the bodice and hem. A matching ribbon gathered the material beneath her breasts. A lacy parasol, also trimmed with red ribbon, lay waiting upon the bed, ready for the moment when she exited the room.

She stared at her reflection in the vanity mirror. Should Kenton refuse to take her to wife, it might set her free to marry Robert West, but at too great a price. Troubled eyes mocked her from the glass, and she frowned, arranging a dark curl to grace the column of her throat.

Only today did she realise just what she had jeopardised in order to meet Robert: the financial security of her family. Breakfast this morning had been intolerable, as she had witnessed her parents' glee. She hardly knew how she'd face them should the earl's decision be unfavourable.

Reaching for the rouge pot, she applied a trace to her pale cheekbones with a soft hare's foot. She frowned again, knowing she could do nothing more to improve her appearance. The spark had fled her eyes and there was precious little she could do to make it return.

A brief knock sounded on her door, and Katie, a veritable tempest, stormed into the room. She barely waited until the door latched shut before launching into a scornful, "Hah! I am now assured that Major West is indeed a rake, a lech—a blackguard of the first degree!"

Claire sat rooted in openmouthed astonishment.

"You will never guess!" Katie spat out. "I saw him on Bond Street, pretty as you please, dancing attendance on some female of *questionable* morals. He is the *lowest,* the most *despicable—*"

It couldn't be true! Robert would never! Her face a frozen mask, Claire drew upon all her dignity to muster a faltering "I'm sure you must be mistaken, Katie."

"I am not mistaken. It was Robert West, as sure as I'm standing here. I waited until the woman had disappeared inside a shop and spoke with him, telling him exactly what I thought of him and his actions. He has used you in the most fiendish manner—why, I could cheerfully box his ears!"

Claire turned again to the mirror, making a pretext of adjusting the red ribbon in her hair. She forced herself to subdue a rapid pulse and breathe normally. Katie had seen Robert, with another woman no less, and spoken with him? She sighed, lacking the heart to argue and the inclination to pursue the details. She summoned a smile. "Well, since Robert West is nothing to me, I can't see what the fuss is about."

Katie looked momentarily deflated, if a slackened lower lip was any indication of her feelings. Recovering her poise, she said coolly, "The Earl of Kenton must be a tolerant and generous man. I wonder he didn't box

West's ears himself when he caught you with him in Hyde Park!''

Claire whirled from the mirror. Speechless, she clutched the folds of her gown to steady her trembling hands.

Katie sniffed, spreading her fingers in an apologetic gesture. "I was going to follow you, but when I saw his lordship trailing you, well, I reasoned my presence wasn't needed. And it's a good thing I waited, Claire, because Smithers locked the door not a minute after I sneaked back inside!''

Claire sank down on her bed, a hand automatically reaching for her parasol to give it occupation. She expelled a long, pent-up breath. "Then I am beholden to you, Katie. Thank you." Casting her sister an agonised glance, she whispered, "His lordship isn't sure he wants to marry me now.''

"Lord have mercy," whispered Katie, plopping onto a nearby chair. "I never thought... It didn't once cross my mind to intercept him.''

"It's not your fault. I should never have gone. But I did, and now I am awaiting his decision." She shrugged. "Mayhap he will accept me still, and I needn't breathe a word of this to Mama and Papa. 'Tis all I can hope for.''

The clatter of horses' hooves sounded on the cobblestones below, and Claire gave a startled jump. The parasol slid from her nerveless fingers. She and Katie raced as one to the window, watching the Earl of Kenton alight from his phaeton and toss the reins to his tiger. He strode purposefully to the gate, lifted the latch and clanked it into place behind him with a decisive flick of his wrist.

The sombre hue of his attire emphasised his grim and forbidding air. Claire exchanged a glance with her sister, fearing her eyes betrayed her anxiety. Katie patted her arm in sympathy and concern. Claire straightened her shoulders and retrieved her parasol, marching to the door. "Well, he can't kill me."

THE DISTANCE to Hyde Park was covered in silence, silence which Claire, sitting primly with her parasol unfurled, passed by observing the earl and his trappings of wealth. She noted the lightness with which his slender, gloved fingers handled the reins. His team of matched greys were beautifully trained, responding to his slightest command. They were also some of the finest horseflesh Claire had ever seen. Expense and breeding were evident from the fine pointed tips of their ears to the plumed tails swishing against their hocks. The phaeton, too, stated affluence in a quiet, unpretentious manner. It was shiny black, adorned with delicate tracings of silver.

Her eyes moved to his lordship's person. Black Hessian boots gave way to muscled thighs encased in doeskin. His bottle-green coat could have come from only one source: Weston himself. Excellent tailoring and elegant simplicity were apparent in every stitch.

Claire recalled the shopping done for herself, for a comeout of the cheapest order. Her mother had sifted through materials for the best bargains, counting every farthing spent. The dressmaker, though acceptable, wasn't in the least fashionable. Claire had relied upon her own deft fingers and *La Belle Assemblée* to add those fripperies necessary for her modish gowns. She recognized all of a sudden that she hadn't a clue as to the extent of his lordship's wealth, and wondered just as swiftly if she would be sharing it. His silence was becoming unnerving.

"I trust a wedding date set for ten days hence will be acceptable to you?"

His calm, unpertubed tones made her straighten with a jerk. Ten days! Merciful heavens! Her stomach constricted in a tight knot. Her lashes flew up, and for a moment, she indulged in the unladylike act of staring. His cool, grey gaze slid slowly over her face then flicked forward again as he manoeuvred his team through the gates of the Park. His finely molded lips quirked into what she construed as a smug smile; no doubt he was satisfied at having put her wits all about! Anger flared with a swift burst of energy. Of all the toplofty, arrogant—!

Oh, yes, your high and mightiness! she wanted to snap, but the sudden thought that she *should* feel grateful for his generosity stayed her tongue. She drew a deep breath, seeking to quell her temper. "Your magnanimity has been duly noted, my lord," she said, unable to squelch the rancour in her tone. "I'm sure 'twould be unforgivable of me if I didn't fall sweetly into your plans."

A snapping of twin black brows rewarded her. His blazing eyes sought to lock with hers, and though she quivered inside, she refused to flinch. Slowly, a grin quirked his lips.

"It's gratifying to know I've chosen so biddable a bride."

His sarcasm wasn't lost on her, but Claire found she had no suitable rejoinder. Though he laughed at her, that one lift of his sensual lip made her heart lurch, and it took her a moment to catch her breath.

She didn't care to analyse why a simple grin should affect her so, concluding simply that she had rarely seen him smile. Acknowledging his remark with a stately dip of her head, Claire looked away, only to have her calm facade shattered by the sight of Major Robert West.

He looked haggard, as if he hadn't slept well. A trace of beard shadowed his face. Claire hoped he wasn't pining for her; she'd feel awful if he were. He rode toward them on his big bay gelding. Her heart hammered, and she knew a twinge of pride for the courage he must require to face his lordship. Robert acknowledged her with a low bow from the saddle. Her lips lifted tentatively in return.

"I trust the day finds you well, Miss Dempsey?" he enquired, after the briefest of nods towards the earl.

"Very well, I thank you. And you?" She was dismayed to hear the tremble in her voice. Her breath was behaving in the most erratic fashion.

He nodded an affirmation. "Indeed. I've received my marching orders. I shall be out of Town for some time." His gaze slid to the earl, and back to her. "I owe you an apology, Miss Dempsey. And you, Kenton. I beg forgiveness of you both."

Claire was quick to voice hers, though Nicolas merely gave an abrupt nod. Her attention returned to Major West. "I wish you good luck," she said softly, a hint of concern in her voice.

"Thank you. I wish you the same." His gaze locked with hers for one brief second, then snapped to Kenton's. They exchanged a glare. Robert lifted his hand in a final salute and clicked the bay forward, cantering away with Claire's heart and her last hope of a happy future.

She peeked at Nicolas, seeking his reaction at meeting Robert after the contretemps of last night. His face was an inscrutable mask. He swivelled a level grey glance at her beneath his lashes and she looked away, receiving the impression that he wasn't at all put out.

A deft flick of his wrists urged the matched greys forward again through the press of carriages and horse-

men. The haut ton was out in force to see and be seen.
Claire recalled his lordship's words of the previous evening...something about privacy? The remark was
laughable.

She glanced about, intercepting the envious frowns
bestowed upon her by a sniffing matron and her missish
daughter. She might as well become used to such looks,
for Society would soon know of their betrothal. The announcement, Sir Percival had informed her at breakfast,
would be in the morning's *Gazette*.

A queer little shiver sliced through her. This morning
that possibility had seemed unlikely. Now the reality of
it came near to cracking her composure. She gazed at
Kenton, noting his lean, supple face, the strong jaw, and
lashes that looked longer in profile. Ten days would see
her wed to this man. The thought was unnerving.

His gaze flickered towards her, and hers shied away.
The green of the Park, the bright colours of those making the fashionable parade, the horses, the carriages...
all swam together in one blurred kaleidoscope. She was
painfully aware she'd been staring again.

"Miss Dempsey," he said, a hint of mirth colouring his
tones, "I assure you, I take no umbrage in your accus-
toming yourself to my countenance. I do believe the more
familiar I become to you, the less frightening you will
find me."

"I'm not frightened of you, my lord," Claire stated,
her fingers curling round the stem of her parasol. She
noted the glance he bestowed on the action, and realised
she clutched it as if it were a lifeline. With a small sigh,
she relaxed her grip.

"I find that information gratifying," he returned, a
dry smile playing across his lips. "And I'll be more satisfied when you cease my lording me, and call me Nico-

las. I daresay my mama will be shocked if she finds we're not yet on a first-name basis.''

''Your mama?'' Claire squeaked, her heart tripping faster at the thought of the Countess of Kenton.

''Yes, my mama. She's quite eager to meet you. If you've had your fill of doing the pretty here, I suggest we go so I may perform the introductions. I dislike having to rush you, but we have much to do in a very short time. I shall be leaving Town this evening.''

''You're leaving Town this evening, my lord?'' Claire echoed, stunned. ''Why so?''

He hesitated, his lashes descending, guarding his expression. ''I must put my estate in order to receive my bride, of course.''

She frowned, unable to imagine the Earl of Kenton letting anything get out of order. He was hiding something, she made sure. A thought struck her. She tried to dislodge the sinking feeling that he'd taken an aversion to her, but the idea wouldn't be banished. ''Of course. And when do you hope to return, m'lord?''

''It's Nicolas, remember? And I doubt I'll return until the evening before we marry.''

''And am I to arrange all the details of this wedding by post...Nicolas?'' she questioned, suddenly peevish. Her intended would not be dancing attendance on her, and the wedding was but ten days off! Surely she had the right to expect some of his attention!

His enigmatic eyes slid over her. ''The details of the wedding need not concern you overmuch. I've given my mother precise instructions, and she's delighted to be of help in this matter. I rather thought all the haste would try your nerves, so I've asked her to alleviate every burden she may. Of course, there will be your trousseau to choose, and several other matters which only you can decide.''

Resentment flooded Claire. How she despised him! It wasn't enough that he had waltzed into her life, upsetting her every dream for the future. Then, he must have the *audacity* to catch her in a midnight tryst with the man she loved, the *arrogance* to be angry just because she was betrothed to him, and the *presumption* to arrange the details of her wedding without consulting her!

Conscience smote her. He *had* kept her actions from her parents' ears. He *had* behaved the gentleman. He *hadn't* released her from the engagement, nor allowed her reputation to be ruined. She should feel thankful, even relieved, but she couldn't like the way he was ordering her life.

''I must remember to thank her for her generosity. It's most kind of her to offer her help,'' she said demurely. The Countess of Kenton. She didn't relish the prospect of meeting her. The woman must be a forbidding creature indeed, to have raised such a son.

A brief smile lifted his lips. ''I doubt her intentions are anything but kind, for she'd move heaven and earth to see me standing at the altar.'' He chuckled, a low sound coming from deep in his throat, pleasing to her ears. ''I'm sure you'll like her, and she is kind, don't mistake me... but, I would be more inclined to describe her as flighty.''

The affectionate cast of his features banished the hint of austere hauteur. So the man had a heart, after all. Would she ever penetrate his barriers and touch it? Remembering his opinions on affection, Claire doubted it was possible. She also doubted she'd want to.

"You're strangely quiet, Miss Dempsey," he remarked, manoeuvring his team neatly through the Park gates.

Claire chewed on her bottom lip, searching for words. "My lord, I wasn't sure we'd be wed until some few minutes ago. Now you inform me the date is set for ten days hence, that you will be leaving Town, and that your mother will be the one I need apply to. I didn't know you had a mother, and I don't even know where your estate is located."

She blew a frustrated puff of air through her teeth. "Forgive my complaints, but shouldn't I have a clue as to what my future holds? I cannot understand all this haste, why you're so eager to be wed and to cart me off to God knows where. I'm sure I wouldn't take it amiss if you could find it in your heart to enlighten me."

"How remiss of me," he acknowledged, dropping the reins and bringing his team to a halt. "Of course you have every right to know where we shall reside—it's just north of Dover. My mother, I'm sure, will fill you in on any other details of my life. As to the haste of this marriage—" a slender finger lifted her chin and he looked straight into her eyes "—I need an heir. As soon as possible."

Sudden fear mingled with shy uncertainty. Claire's face grew hot, and she dropped her gaze to her lap. Her mother had educated her on the duties of marriage just that day, but only now did the full impact of the idea besiege her. Dear Lord, she would...they would...she dared not think on it. The heat of his lordship's finger warmed her chin. She forced herself to return his penetrating scrutiny. "I see."

He nodded briefly, dropped his finger and lifted the reins. "My mother will put her carriage at your disposal. I hope you won't find it too onerous if she insists on accompanying you everywhere, and helping where she may. She's so delighted that I've finally chosen a bride that I fear wild horses couldn't keep her from being at your beck and call. She's a whirlwind, but I've given her strict instructions not to wear you out."

"Your solicitude is heart-warming," Claire said, unable to keep a hint of waspishness from her tones. Famous! A managing mama, and a managing son. Not at all what she'd reckoned on.

Kenton cast her a glance, his brows furrowed. "You're sure you haven't had enough for one day?"

"Positive, my lord." She'd endured it all today. Why not meet her future mother-in-law, as well? Claire bit her tongue, praying for fortitude.

The earl pulled up before a modish town house and jumped to the ground, tossing the reins to his tiger. Claire had forgotten the lad, and was embarrassed at what he may have overheard. She watched, bemused, as Kenton gesticulated with his hands and moved his mouth slowly, though no sound issued forth. The boy nodded, and appearing satisfied, Kenton turned away, lifting his arms to help her from the phaeton.

"He's deaf," he replied to Claire's questioning look, and grinned. "I couldn't ask for a more discreet servant."

Claire returned his smile, intrigued at his kind patience towards the boy. 'Twas the second time today she'd glimpsed a softer side of Nicolas. For the first time in her life, she perceived her five-foot-five-inch frame as delicate. The hands she rested on his shoulders for support transmitted the whipcord strength of the muscles beneath his coat. Before she could expel a breath, her feet touched the ground. He offered his arm and they made their way to the massive front portal.

The door swung open before they reached the top step. A stately butler bowed low. "Your lordship, your mother awaits you in the Green Salon."

"Thank you, Clark. Please meet my future bride, Miss Claire Dempsey. Claire, Clark will accompany us upon our remove to Dover."

The butler made another very correct and proper bow, expressing his pleasure in meeting her. Claire smiled, acknowleding the introduction. Kenton's hand on her elbow guided her forward, towards what she supposed was the Green Salon, and the unknown entity awaiting her.

She scarce had time to register the muted-green-and-apricot decor of the salon before the tiny figure seated in an overstuffed chair launched herself at them. The Countess of Kenton was all of five feet tall, Claire guessed, and had the neatest little figure she'd ever seen on a woman of matronly years. Her dark hair, cropped close à la Titus, displayed a pleasing combination of silver entwined with black. Fashionably attired and pretty, she had dark eyes which shone with warmth and interest. All this Claire assimilated before the countess gathered her into a tight embrace.

"Oh, Nicolas! Is this your Claire?" Leaning back, she surveyed her son's intended and emitted a delighted gurgle. "Why, my darling, you are simply beautiful! Nicolas, I congratulate you on your choice!"

Claire noted the twinkle in his lordship's eyes. "Yes, Mama," he said, his voice holding a hint of amusement, "this is Claire, and thank you."

"Dearest Claire—I may call you that, mayn't I? Why, I vow your beauty takes my breath away! Nicolas, do ring for Clark. I've been holding tea for you, and I shan't wait a moment longer! Dearest, do come and sit down.'' She drew Claire to a small sofa and sat beside her, nearly quivering with excitement. ''Nicolas tells me your mother is Mary Stanley. She was a beauty in her day, so I shouldn't be surprised at your loveliness. I can't tell you how it pleases me to welcome you to the family, and how very delighted I am that my dear son has *finally*—''

''Mama, I daresay you should draw a breath now,'' drawled Nicolas, his mouth quirking in a grin.

For the first time, Claire noticed the even whiteness of his teeth. He lounged against the mantel, one arm carelessly braced against the marble. He looked powerfully handsome and...virile? Claire barely believed she would describe him thus, and flicked her gaze away, angry for thinking such a thing of him.

The countess emitted a tinkling laugh, bestowing a tender glance on her son. ''Ah, yes, I do forget one must occasionally have air. Now do tell, Claire, has Nicolas informed you he must leave Town? Personally, I think it's the outside of enough, and told him so. He insists, however, that he must go. So, by your leave, we shall have the greatest fun preparing a wedding grand enough for the Earl of Kenton and his countess. Of course, I shall insist your mama accompany us, for you are her first chick to fly the nest. I warned Nicolas that he'll be sorry for leaving his purse in our hands—''

''Ah,'' interjected Nicolas, cocking his head. ''I do believe I hear Clark approaching with the tea.''

Claire glanced from him to the animated countenace of his mother. She was rather intrigued at the change in Nicolas's demeanour. He seemed relaxed and in good humour. It also surprised her that his mother should be such a chatterbox. What a delightful and refreshing change the countess was from her son. Not at all what Claire had expected.

Clark brought in the tea tray, and Nicolas strolled over, pulling a chair nearer the tea table and far too close to herself. One doeskin-clad knee grazed her thigh, but Claire resisted the impulse to draw away. Certain he tried to put her out of countenance, she refused to rise to the bait.

"My lady, I vow my mother and I will greatly appreciate your help," Claire ventured, watching her pour out the tea. "As the wedding is to be in a mere ten days, I'm sure we shan't be able to plan fast enough."

The countess smiled warmly. "Call me Fanny, my dear. And yes, I agree ten days shows unseemly haste, but there you have it. Nicolas, dear boy though he is, hasn't the least concern for marrying in style. It's as well he called me to Town. I fear he'd have settled for some sloppy chapel on Fleet Street. Now, I hope the tea is to your liking, and please, have one of these cucumber sandwiches. Nicolas's cook is a marvel...."

Nicolas relaxed in his chair, content to let his mother chatter whilst he covertly studied Claire. He could have kicked himself for not complimenting her appearance when he'd arrived to collect her, but the truth of it was, she'd quite taken his breath away.

White and red were perfect adjuncts to her colouring, and even now, he found his gaze drawn to her creamy throat and the dark lock caressing it. He wondered how many times in the past hour he'd wished his fingertips were stroking that silky curl, and how many times he'd had the impulse to brush it aside.

A stirring deep within warned him his thoughts were getting out of line. *Gather yourself, Kenton,* he admonished. It was as well he wouldn't be seeing her until the wedding. She was enough to heat a monk's blood.

He caught the sharp glance she cast his way, and nearly laughed aloud. Miss Claire Dempsey had shown him a side today he hadn't known she possessed. Here was no milk-and-water miss, prepared to curtsy at his slightest whim. Odd, that fact hadn't struck him sooner—he should have realised it last night when she went scampering off to meet Robert West.

Had he made a dangerous mistake in believing she would be a demure, quiet wife? Life with her, he made sure, wouldn't be boring, but it might prove to be most uncomfortable. He hoped she was one of those chits who kept to her own business, and prayed she slept like a baby at night. And thinking of babies, she hadn't looked terribly thrilled at the thought of bearing his.

"Now, I daresay I should allow Nicolas to return you to your family," said his mother, bringing him from his musings.

He sat forward and replaced his cup on the tray, noticing the grace of Claire's movements as she did the same, and the pretty smile she bestowed upon his mother. Would she ever smile upon him in like fashion? Doubtful. And why this perturbed little feeling wiggling through him?

"My carriage shall be at your disposal at ten," his mother told Claire. "I do hope that's not too early? I vow we'll be horribly busy, but I've promised Nicolas not to present him with a drooping bride. We must be sure you have time to rest before the event."

Some fifteen minutes later, Nicolas escorted Claire up the stairs of her home. He refused her invitation to step inside. "I've many miles to go this evening, and I daresay I should be on my way."

He took the hand she offered, his gaze skimming her face. She looked beautiful, and he would have liked to say so, but the cool expression in her green eyes stayed his tongue. He doubted she'd appreciate his belated compliments. Instead, he contented himself with the brief words, "I hope the next ten days pass well with you."

"Thank you, m'lord," Claire graciously replied. Bemused at the day's events, she watched in some perplexity his return to his phaeton. The next time she met him, they would be at the altar. She dreaded the prospect.

CHAPTER FIVE

NICOLAS REGARDED THE MAN seated opposite him with a look just short of a glare. He wished he could shake the wretch until his teeth rattled, but, of course, that would never do. Personal prejudices must be laid aside if they were to return Andrew to English soil. He stood, walking to the sideboard and the decanter set atop it. "Brandy, Major West?"

"Thank you," came Robert's short reply.

Nicolas unstopped the decanter, feeling West's gaze boring into his back. They clearly disliked each other with an equal intensity, if West's animosity, thinly veiled with politeness, was any indication. West wasn't about to make amends, that much was apparent.

Perhaps West had a hint of steel in his character, after all. Nicolas considered this whilst he filled two glasses and stopped the decanter. He'd best not let past differences colour his judgement. He knew too little about Major Robert West.

Handing a glass to West, he resumed his chair. Gazing thoughtfully over the rim of his own, he tried to discern the silent messages emanating from his cohort. The major seemed at ease, lounging with booted ankles crossed before him. But a certain rigidity in the way he held his glass, and indeed, his body, suggested an entirely different state of mind: a marked tenseness, a definite wariness, a constant alertness.

"Major West," Nicolas began, rubbing his thumbs against the smooth surface of his glass. "There's a great deal to be done, and our time is limited. It's abundantly clear we have little regard for each other, but we cannot allow that...unfortunate fact to stand in the way of our mission. During these next days, I'll show you how our operation works, and I must insist on having your full cooperation."

"Indeed," drawled West, a corner of his mouth curling up.

"Your enthusiasm quite lays my fears to rest," Nicolas returned in like manner, mimicking the curled upper lip. He surveyed the other man, noting that another day's growth of beard shadowed his face. "Now that I rest easy on that score, I trust you brought a suitable wardrobe?"

"If dirty, stinking and reeking of poverty is what you mean, yes. Renshaw adjured me to give you no cause for upset. Your wish is my command."

"Gratified to hear it. In return, I shall do all in my power to see you fully equipped to escape that rat hole of France alive. My knowledge is yours...please don't hesitate to tap it." His lip lifted wryly, and was immediately masked by the rim of his glass.

"I shall see that you move as silently as a cat," Nicolas continued, "that you have a thorough knowledge of where you're going and where I suspect Andrew to be. We'll clear points of rendezvous, and you'll be given intimate knowledge of my secret cave. I expect you to seek refuge here when you return, unless, of course, someone is following you.

"I regret being a poor host—" again his lips curled "—but the chances of your being seen and recognised would be greatly multiplied were you to have a guest chamber. I'm afraid the servants' quarters below-stairs will be your lot. You may rely upon my groom John, Clark, my butler, and Mrs. Trumble, the house-keeper. Otherwise, I expect discretion to be observed.''

Robert's lips thinned. "Afraid I'll dally with your maids, Kenton?''

Nicolas regarded him with distaste. "No. But our villains are Englishmen, spying for the French. There's no telling what connections they may have here. I daresay survival dictates we keep as close as possible. Any other questions?''

"Not as yet, I'm sure," Robert replied, his gaze flicking over Nicolas in acute dislike. "But I shan't hesitate to ask should one occur to me.''

"I'm sure you won't. I've no doubts you'll be a joy to work with, Major. Our beginning has proved most... shall we say, *promising?* In light of our mutual regard, I have but one more request to make of you. Should you come into contact with Miss Dempsey, at any time, for any reason, do remember that we will be married, therefore, I insist you respect her *as my fiancée,* and treat her accordingly.''

Robert's lips lifted in a cocky half smile. "Ah, I wondered when you'd get round to that. Come, Kenton. It's obvious you have little respect for my morals, and even less for my person. Rather humorous, don't you think, that we're placed in a position where we must *trust* each other?''

"Quite," was Nicolas's chopped reply. *Insolent bastard,* he thought.

West swirled the liquid about in his glass, lifted it and tossed off the final swallow. "The biggest difference between us, Kenton, is that you were born heir to an earl, and I was born but a nephew to one. My uncle's money bought my colours, just as your money bought you a wife."

"That's the way of the world, West. The rich man marries the beautiful woman, and all others keep their hands off."

"Rather galling to know, isn't it," West replied, "that your wife is in love with another man?"

"Rather galling to know, isn't it," Nicolas answered, "that the woman you love will marry another man?"

"Ah, but *I* didn't buy her—I won her. All your riches won't purchase her love, Kenton. Yours is a rather hollow victory, if you don't mind my saying so."

Nicolas regarded him coldly. This reminder of his greatest attraction for women did nothing to endear West to him. For a few brief moments, he despised the man more than the traitors who sought his life. Clamping a firm hold on his animosity, he responded icily, "Rather villainous, don't you suppose, to win her regard, and leave her a heartbroken widow?"

"I had no idea I'd stand in danger of leaving her widowed so early," West shot back. "Unlike you."

"Ah, but I won't leave her a *heartbroken* widow. I'll leave her a *rich* one." Nicolas's stomach twisted at the sheer truth of these words, though he couldn't fathom why. It had nothing to do with the thought of his demise.

"And ideally with your heir planted in her belly?" Robert sneered.

"God willing, yes." Nicolas rose, setting his glass aside. Another minute of this conversation and he would give West the throttling he so desired to inflict. "If we're in perfect understanding of each other, I suggest we set about the business at hand. I have much to teach. You have much to learn. And the days are short."

"WILL YOU JOIN ME in a glass of sherry, m'dear?" asked Fanny, Countess of Kenton, scarcely moments after Claire was ushered into the Green Salon of the Kenton town house. "I always say a spot of sherry in the morning is most uplifting to the spirits. It soothes the nerves and puts a smile on the face. I daresay your internals profit, too."

Claire wondered how she could refuse in the face of this logic, even though a glass of sherry sounded revolting. She would much have preferred a cup of chocolate, but instead smiled graciously. "Thank you, my lady."

"Do have a seat, Claire, and tell me why your mama hasn't accompanied you."

"Mama sends her regrets and apologies to your ladyship." Claire gathered the skirts of her ice blue gown, and sank onto an overstuffed chair upholstered in pale green and apricot stripes. "She's having the veriest spasms over my wedding gown, and vows she cannot trust the maids to do a proper job of laundering it. She insists on overseeing the operation, declaring her old dress is hardly suitable for the Countess of Kenton, in any case."

"Fustian! You'd look every inch the countess did you wear rags!" Lady Kenton turned from the sideboard. Skirts swishing, she proffered the glass of golden liquid.

"Thank you, my lady," Claire shyly responded, peering into the liquid with decided misgivings. "Papa said much the same, but that's small consolation to Mama. She asked if you would come to tea this afternoon, to discuss the wedding plans."

"I shall be delighted. And you must remember to call me Fanny, dear. I am so beleaguered with all this 'Countess,' and 'your ladyship' and 'Lady Kenton' that sometimes I think if I didn't talk to myself, I would forget my name! I vow Nicolas's father was the last to use it, and that's been near five years. Such a sorry pass, as I rather like being called Fanny.''

"It suits you admirably." Claire touched the rim of the glass to her lips. "I'll try to address you as such, but you must know it seems rather uncomfortable, as you are Nicolas's mother."

"Of course, but I am hardly so formidable, am I?" Fanny emitted a tinkling laugh. "Unfortunate, perhaps, as I understand a countess is supposed to be very high in the instep, but there you have it."

"Oh, not at all unfortunate!" Claire responded with intensity. "In truth, I am relieved! From what I know of Nicolas, I own I rather feared you'd be int..." She trailed off miserably, heat rising in her face. A hasty gulp of sherry slid smoothly down her throat. She decided the drink wasn't so bad after all.

Fanny tilted back her head, gurgling appreciatively. "Oh, you mustn't be put out of countenance, my dear. I can't tell you how gratified I am to hear you say so! Though I love him dearly, my poor Nicolas can sometimes be so... stuffy. Oh, never so with his family, of course, for there he can be quite tolerant, but with the ladies! I vow I despaired of seeing him wed—at least to a woman who is *human*."

At Claire's questioning expression, she sighed. Her eyes narrowed thoughtfully, and she spread her hands in a gesture of acceptance. "I doubt Nicolas's forgiveness should I relate this story, and you mustn't say I told you so; however, I feel you have every right to know why he sometimes appears so, how shall we say it... austere?"

Claire's ears perked with interest. She nodded the tiniest encouragement.

"Well," Fanny said, scooting forward on her chair, "to look at him now, you wouldn't guess Nicolas was once quite...*charming*." She giggled at the lifting of Claire's brows. "Yes, he was charming. Oh, he's always been rather serious, but I vow he could laugh with the best of them."

Her eyes grew pensive, and interested in spite of herself, Claire leaned closer.

"He fell in love at three-and-twenty. She had the face of an angel teamed, alas, with a scheming heart. How prettily she could dimple at him, and she often did, giving him every encouragement."

Claire watched the play of emotions chase across the countess's face, intrigued at this deeper side of the flighty, effervescent Fanny. She wasn't sure Nicolas would care to discover she had this knowledge, either, but she was curious, and couldn't wait to hear the rest.

"Nicolas was captivated. He prepared to speak to the lady's father, certain he couldn't want for a better wife. But one night at a ball, he overheard her discussing the merits of her suitors."

Fanny paused, taking a dainty sip of sherry. "She ranked him among the most preferable, being heir to an earldom, with prospects of great wealth. However, he wasn't yet the earl, and who knew when his papa might stick his spoon in the wall? Neither could she like his penchant for country life, but rather thought his money would make up for any hardship she might suffer. Can you imagine a young miss being so *calculating?*"

Claire's fine brows drew together in disbelief, and she shook her head.

"Nicolas was, of course, devastated. His lily-white angel was nothing but a coldhearted schemer." She sipped her sherry, looking sad. "He was better off without the minx, but became grim and cynical about the purity of the female heart. He believes he's wanted for nothing but his money, and I can't convince him otherwise."

Claire hoped her face hadn't paled. She was one with the scheming minx. Wasn't she marrying Nicolas solely for his money? She couldn't vouch for the purity of her heart, either.

Fanny drained her glass, set it aside and looked intently at Claire. "I know yours isn't a love match, dear," she said softly. "I sometimes wonder if Nicolas will allow himself to feel such affection again. Perhaps, however, you will understand why he appears so cold, and why I'm delighted you aren't the hard, grasping female I feared he'd choose. I can't think you're comfortable with the idea of marrying him, and I'm certainly not asking you to love him, but I do wish you the best with him."

"Thank you, your ladyship," Claire said quietly. She sat back, cradling her glass in her hands. The icy-eyed earl in the throes of unrequited love? She felt pity for him. "I'd like to assure you that Nicolas and I will deal famously, but . . . I fear we scarcely know each other."

"And how could you?" Fanny asked, her brows rising. "I've never seen a quicker courtship and marriage! Why, I almost wish Nicolas were still in leading strings so I could smack his backside. There's no understanding him. He suddenly takes a notion it's time to find a wife, and *voilà!* He secures her hand and runs off to the country without so much as a by-your-leave! It's too havey-cavey in my opinion, and I vow I'd be most offended were I you."

She sniffed, then brightened. "Well, we'd best not mope on this subject any longer, lest we find ourselves needing another sherry restorative. Come along with me." She led the way out of Green Salon, her skirts rustling.

Claire followed, shaking her head and smiling at the countess's mercurial change of mood.

"The best way to learn a man's character is to look at his home," Fanny said. "What colours does he surround himself with...are his servants well trained? Are they happy or surly? What are his inclinations in furnishings and art? I bade my daughters to watch carefully, lest they shackle themselves to a man with no refinement. I'm happy to say you shan't find Nicolas lacking in taste."

Over the next hour, she regaled Claire with stories of Nicolas's childhood, interspersing the tales with illustrations of his refinement and character, all leavened by her lighthearted humour.

They traipsed from the scullery to Nicolas's bedchamber, the latter bringing a queer flutter to Claire's breast. The decor was simple, yet rich, done in navy blue and beige, and once again, Claire wondered how he contrived that atmosphere of unostentatious wealth. The huge bed, hung with navy silk, brought her all too close to the thought of sleeping with him. She blushed, wishing to escape from the room post-haste.

Fanny, as if sensing her discomfiture, took her arm again. "Well, if I've convinced you my son hasn't a vice, I suggest we have a light repast, scratch out some invitations and join your mama for tea. I do hope she won't take overmuch trouble on my behalf—I daresay her nerves are as aflutter as mine were when my daughters married. Has Nicolas told you of his two sisters?"

Nicolas, Claire thought, had told her nothing. Until today, she hadn't realised how very little she knew about him. And she didn't dislike what she'd learned. His mother obviously loved him dearly. She murmured an appropriate response to Fanny, following her into a bright and sunny breakfast parlour.

OVER TEA, Lady Dempsey and the countess drew up a monumental list of tasks needing to be accomplished for a wedding befitting the Earl of Kenton and his countess. The following morning, plans continued to unfold, with the most important item on the list being Claire's trousseau. She shyly voiced the opinion that she couldn't like spending a great deal of his lordship's money, but Fanny soon set her straight.

"My dear!" she admonished. "Nicolas has commissioned me to see you dressed in the finest of fashion. Besides, you shall be married to the man and spending his money for the rest of your life. You may as well become used to it."

Claire, failing to conjure a single argument in the face of this reasoning, allowed the countess to guide her and her female relatives to the best modiste in Town. Deirdre and Delight nearly went wild with ecstasy.

"Oh, do look at these fabrics, Delight!" Deirdre squealed. "Why, I vow there's every colour under the sun! Oh, dear me, I can't *wait* until the day I marry. I shall choose *everything!*"

"Not unless your husband is as rich as the earl," said Katie in an undertone the countess couldn't hear, though she and Lady Dempsey were already speaking with the modiste.

"Oh, I assure you," Deirdre solemnly responded, "my husband shall be *very* rich. I shan't marry him if he's not."

"Don't you care for love, sister dear?" Claire asked, her heart regretful that she herself hadn't any choice but to marry money.

"Love?" scoffed Deirdre. "Really, Claire, I should hope not. Why, in one romance I read, the silly heroine spurned the *richest* man for some poor farmer, which I thought foolish above half. Whyever should you settle for a cottage instead of a mansion?"

"Deirdre," said Delight, "I would have been furious had she not married the farmer! I vow I shouldn't want to marry some poxy old man just because he has *money*. Really!"

"Delight," Deirdre returned, "I have no intentions of marrying a poxy old man. I daresay I can find someone young, as well as rich. Claire did. At least, I suppose his lordship is young to her, though I rather think he's too old for me. But when I'm old enough to marry, I imagine the men will seem younger. Don't you agree? And Delight, we must be sure to dress *exactly* alike in our Season. Think of the fun we'll have setting the Town on its ear, wondering which of us is which!"

"You'll get yourselves in a great deal of trouble," Katie warned.

"Oh, but it will be so worth it!" laughed Delight.

Claire exchanged a glance with Katie, well knowing the twins' mischievous natures and how likely they would be to pull off such a stunt. "It's to be hoped," she said in a dry aside to Katie, "that they'll grow up before they're presented."

"Indeed," Katie agreed.

"Claire," Delight said in a awestruck whisper, indicating a fashion plate. "You must have this gown. I vow you'd look stunning!"

"Oh, no, she must have this one," cried Deirdre, pointing to another.

"She shall have both," proclaimed Fanny, joining them with Lady Dempsey and the modiste in tow.

"Claire, madame should like to take your measurements, then we shall get to the task of choosing. Let's see ... you shall need a travelling costume, a ball gown made up in that silver gauze and a riding habit. I do hope you like to ride. Nicolas is so keen on the sport...."

Claire allowed the modiste to lead her off to a fitting room. Afterwards, patterns and material flew at her from all angles. Never before had she seen such finery, and never before had she such a free hand to spend so much money! She laughingly exclaimed that his lordship would rue the day he set eyes on her. A bit of the devil took her at the private thought that he'd bought her for a wife, so he might as well pay for the privilege.

The morning passed in a whirl, as did the next seven days. All the bustle made it easy to push the Earl of Kenton from her mind, until the night before her wedding. As she sank into bed, the reality of her situation struck her. Tomorrow she would marry him. She shuddered at the thought and wrapped the blankets more closely about her. The countess was a dear, making it hard to believe Nicolas was her son.

An image of his lordship swam before her closed eyes. She bade it flee. Tomorrow was soon enough; indeed, far *too* soon to become the bride of a man who hadn't the decency to acknowledge her presence by a single note. At a time when most grooms would dance attendance on their ladies, hers had left the scene, showing all the world how little he considered her feelings. Was this the type of behaviour she could expect from him? He couldn't have demonstrated more clearly just how coldblooded a contract they entered.

She couldn't agree with Fanny. His disappearance into the country wasn't at all havey-cavey. There was but one thing which could have taken him from her side during this crucial period before their wedding. She had given him a disgust of herself, and he couldn't abide her presence.

Then why is he marrying you? The question came from nowhere, demanding an answer. She rolled over, giving her pillow a smart rap with her fist. Oh, how should she know? But what other explanation was there for his rag-mannered return to the country? She couldn't accept his story of setting his estate in order.

And what about Fanny's disclosure of his sad affair? He knew she married him solely for his money, so how was it so different from his first love? And after her tryst with Robert, he'd had every reason to break their betrothal. Did he want her for herself? The idea died an instant death. No, he needed that heir—but why all the haste? Something just didn't fit.

She sighed. She'd plague herself no longer with these unanswered questions. The worst part about it was that no matter what his reasons, she was still beholden to him. It would have been worse not to marry him than to marry him. He was bestowing upon her the favour now.

She thought wryly that there was a definite parallel between them. Nicolas's attraction was his money…hers, her beauty. His gold had bought him a wife; her countenance had snared a rich husband. Surely this knowledge of one's value, based solely on outer trappings, was as galling to him as it was to her. Could she take comfort in knowing he'd paid dearly for her looks? Would he find her worth the price?

She rolled over again, wrapping herself deeply in the blankets. She would think no more of the Earl of Kenton. She squeezed her eyes tight, and with a jolt, realised she'd hardly thought of Robert West for more than a week. Deciding all the activity had left no room for anything else, she tried to conjure up his face, thinking to dwell on it just one more night. But as she sank into sleep, it wasn't Robert West's face dancing before her, it was the Earl of Kenton's. Damn his icy eyes!

NICOLAS STOOD with Major West at the mouth of the secret cave which tunnelled from beneath his house to the Strait of Dover. A small craft bobbed in the water, prepared for Robert's journey to France in search of Andrew.

"One more thing, West," Nicolas said, fishing in his pocket, and bringing forth a crooked coin. "Should you find Andrew alive, give him this. He'll know you came from me, and will therefore trust you."

Slowly, West looked the coin over. He quirked a lip. "Does this mean you trust me, as well?"

"Only as much as I have to, Major."

West chuckled, flipped the coin in the air, caught it and sauntered to the rowboat. He pushed off, lifting a final hand in mocking salute.

Nicolas watched with a wry twist to his lips, raising a hand in return. To give him credit, West was an apt pupil. Two days into his training, Nicolas was convinced Renshaw had been correct—as usual. Robert West was just the man to find Andrew. For all his cocky, insolent ways, he was clever, with a quick mind. The fuller beard, hennaed hair and reeking clothes did much to disguise the dashing major in his regimentals of days ago.

Rubbing a hand over his tired eyes, Nicolas prayed God would grant West speed and a fruitful journey. If Andrew was brought out alive, it might mean a quicker ending to Napoleon's rampage.

He sighed. He wished only to seek his bed, but he must return to London, for tomorrow he'd take Miss Claire

Dempsey to wife. He realised he hadn't any idea of where they would marry; his acceptable wife hadn't posted him the details.

His gaze travelled across the water to where West's craft skimmed the surface, taking him out of Claire's life—perhaps forever. But what if West did come back, and what if he, Nicolas, lived to a ripe old age? Was he doing right in taking Claire to wife—or was he coming between two people who truly loved each other?

Yet what if he didn't live to old age, and what if West didn't come back? Claire would be well provided for, as would her family—and his heir, were he blessed with such. But was he being selfish by wedding her when she loved another? And why did it rankle that she did love West? Was he doing right by her—was he doing right by himself? No matter how he'd assured himself he desired no affection, it wasn't easy taking a wife who needed nothing but his gold.

Well, the die was cast, and he could but do his best to be a decent husband, and God willing, to sire a son. Looking heavenward, he shook his head, and straightened his shoulders to meet his future.

CHAPTER SIX

CLAIRE'S HAND trembled in the crook of her father's arm. "Papa," she whispered, "I'm so frightened."

Sir Percival patted her hand, an encouraging smile replacing his cat-in-the-cream grin. "Of course you are, pet. 'Tis natural. I'd be worried if you weren't."

Claire remained unconsoled. Her legs were weak, and her stomach jumped about in a most unsettling manner. The strains of the organ screeched in her ears, and she rather thought she was suffering a severe attack of the nerves.

"There's our cue, daughter. Now hold your head high, as a countess should, and remember, you've done me and your mama proud. I daresay a bride never looked so lovely."

"Thank you, Papa," Claire said, grateful for his attempt to bolster her courage. Her steps automatically fell in with his, and she kept her head high, as he had bidden her. Faces and bonnets blurred before her in a colourful array, and for a brief moment, she wondered if she would manage to reach the altar.

For there stood Nicolas, straight and tall, and looking more formidable than she remembered. A cream-and-pink embroidered waistcoat offset his dove-grey wedding clothes. Katie's bridesmaid gown was exactly the same shade of pink, assuring Claire that Fanny's fingers had meddled in Nicolas's attire. A single, large diamond winked from his snowy cravat, while smaller ones graced the cuffs of his coat.

Black hair, immaculately styled, curled in crisp waves about his face, which appeared leaner and stronger. He looked remote, self-possessed and every inch a peer of the realm. She found herself arrested, however, by the expression in his eyes, which appraised her coolly.

Her chin tilted a touch higher, though her gaze skittered away. The sight of Fanny, her hands clasped rapturously before her, the picture of perfect bliss, restored Claire's confidence. At least his mother liked her.

Nicolas watched his bride s progress. An odd sensation suffused his internals. She looked more beautiful than he remembered. The white gown, embroidered with tiny silver roses, fit her slender figure to perfection. A gauze veil, pinned in the centre of her dark curls, billowed over her creamy shoulders and down her back, giving her the ethereal appearance of an angel. A single strand of pearls adorned her throat, and matching teardrops swayed from shell-perfect ears.

Her expression, however, particularly held his attention. She was frightened, certainly, but something else, too, cautioned him she wasn't in the least bit happy to see him—or to be here at all. He silently cursed Renshaw, Andrew and West for preventing him from courting her more assiduously. He and Miss Claire Dempsey had hardly made an idyllic beginning.

Would she be smiling, her face radiating happiness if it were Robert West she were meeting instead of himself? A knife seemed to twist in his gut. He wasn't her choice of mate, true, but must she hate him because of it? How would they ever rub along if she did?

Sir Percival surrendered to him the care of his daughter. Nicolas executed a tiny, stately bow, accepting

Claire's cold fingers and drawing her forward. The light scent of her perfume wafted to his nostrils, and he inhaled deeper. He cast her a sidelong glance as they knelt before the altar.

The words of the ceremony floated about Claire's head in much the same way as her gauzy veil. To love, to honour, to cherish . . . the vows settled round her ears like a thick London fog. To love? She peeked at Nicolas from under her lashes; he appeared composed and detached. How could she love him? It simply wasn't possible. Dared she voice this ultimate lie? She scarce knew if she made the proper responses; Nicolas's hand holding hers in a light grip became her only reality.

At a slight signal from him, she rose to her feet. Gently, he drew forth her left hand, sliding a twinkling diamond-and-emerald ring onto her third finger.

"I now pronounce you man and wife."

The words rang in her ears like a death knell. Her gaze flew to Nicolas's, locking with his for one terrified moment. His face loomed closer. His lips grazed over hers with the merest touch, the faintest lingering. His breath barely fanned her cheek before he drew away. The contact was so brief, so light that she wondered if she'd been kissed at all. She winced at the mockery of it.

Clearly, he had taken her in disgust. How pressing was his need for an heir that he'd wed a woman he so disliked? It must be great if he would persist in this travesty of a marriage, making vows before God and man. *As had she.*

Tucking her hand in his arm, Nicolas turned her towards the small congregation. A happy smile shone through Fanny's tears. Her mother and sisters looked in much the same condition. And did her father also seem a trifle weepy, or was it her imagination? She didn't have time to be sure. Nicolas guided her back down the aisle, and into the bright sunshine.

The handful of guests poured after them. A small whirlwind flew at Claire, grasping her about the waist. She stumbled backwards, and was caught in the warmth of Nicolas's steadying grip.

"Claire!" cried Percy. "Does this mean I'll never see you again?"

The distress in his voice rang clear and loud in the morning air. Claire leaned towards him, thankful to escape Nicolas's supporting hands. "Oh, no, Percy," she said, hugging him. "It just means I shan't see you as often, that's all. And only think! You'll have one fewer bossy sister to contend with."

Percy cocked his head, considering. "That's true. Very well, then." He turned to Nicolas. "Are you my brother now?"

"Yes, I rather think I am," Nicolas answered, as if considering this circumstance for the first time.

"And will you teach me to drive to an inch?" demanded Percy.

"If you insist." Nicolas's mouth twitched.

"Capital!" whooped Percy, hopping away.

Claire looked at Nicolas, warming at his amused smile. His gaze flicked from Percy's back to her face, and her lashes swooped down. Then Lady Dempsey enfolded her in a tight embrace, and she thankfully transferred her attention from the man who was now her husband.

CLAD IN a deep blue travelling gown, Claire settled back against the soft velvet squabs, revelling in the luxuriously appointed carriage. Silence engulfed her, and she allowed the peace to soothe her jangled nerves.

A row of tall, quiet town houses loomed and receded. Soon London and her past would be left behind; the Dover Road and her future at Kenwood Park lay ahead. That future did not look promising, but it surely could not be any worse than the wedding breakfast they'd just escaped. Far more guests attended the breakfast than the wedding itself, and she couldn't count the number of people she'd greeted and from whom she'd accepted congratulations. Smiling and acting the radiant bride had nearly exhausted her resources. Had Nicolas noticed her composure was about to crack? He'd certainly swept her away as soon as was seemly.

She stole a glance at her newly wedded husband. The term was as foreign to her as the knowledge that she was now his mate. Claire Shea, Countess of Kenton. Her heart jerked with an emotion she couldn't define. Kenton's countess. The wife of the man lounging at ease directly across from her, his face turned to the window so he might observe with supreme casualness those they passed by. He put her in mind of a mediaeval lord, confidently aware he was master of all he surveyed.

His cool grey glance flicked over her face and returned to the scene beyond the window. Certainly *her* master, and she, his chattel. Resentment flared unchecked through her bosom, and she didn't trouble to subdue it when his gaze locked with hers.

Well-formed lips twitched, closing over even white teeth. He sat a bit straighter, drew a deep breath and assessed her with polite detachment. ''I have the impression, lady wife, that not only do you find this marriage distasteful, but that you dislike me, as well. Pray discontinue the pretence. We're alone now, so you may speak freely.''

His quiet, cultured tones fell into the silence like a bee droning for nectar. Claire eyed him for some moments, considering whether she had the audacity to speak her mind. She decided to throw caution to the winds. "You are correct, my lord. I hold you in exceeding dislike."

"And might I ask why... my lady?"

She was reminded of a mouse, pawed about by a merciless cat. That he was her husband cautioned her to show due respect; however, he had asked for honesty. She tilted her chin higher, striving for steady tones. "My parents wished me to marry well, but had you not come along, 'tis possible they might have allowed me to marry where my heart lay. Because of you, I am now destined to spend the remainder of my days in a marriage where there is no love to be given and none to be found."

"Succinctly put," he allowed, inclining his head. "However, I beg leave to inform you, madam, that your beauty had already attracted any number of suitors, many of them as acceptable as I. 'Twas little enough room left for those with nothing to give."

"But you, my lord, are the epitome of virtue in my parents' eyes," she returned, unable to keep bitterness from lacing her voice. "Wealthy, titled, a gentleman of the first rank. I happen to disagree with their notions of what is acceptable in a mate. I feel that having *nothing* but love is far preferable to having *everything* but love."

A fine trace of cynicism showed in the look he bestowed upon her. "Then you are a most singular breed of female" was his flat reply.

She was certain he referred to his unhappy experience with the scheming 'minx', but also knew he didn't know she knew. Hoping to draw him out, she asked with sweet innocence, "How so, my lord? I rather thought all misses hoped for love."

He shook his head. "No, Miss Dempsey, er—" he chuckled and corrected himself "—Lady Kenton. Experience has taught me that most young women marry for two things: material comforts, and to better their position in life. Granted, some marry for love, and others for duty—" he shrugged "—as men do."

"And why, my lord," Claire asked, intrigued, "did you marry? You have no need of money, and surely it wasn't for love."

He gave a short bark of laughter. "Claire, you and I married for the same reason: duty. Your family needed money, mine, a successor to the title."

"You don't care at all for love?" she asked, unable to let the subject drop. She sought something, she knew—that vulnerable, human quality Fanny had assured her he possessed. But there was more she needed to know...why had he chosen her, and why now? "If it were merely an heir you needed, you could have married long ago!"

He studied her for a moment, thick lashes shrouding the expression in his eyes. "Has Mama been telling you my sacred secrets?"

"Oh, n-no!" she stammered, caught off guard. A guilty blush burned her cheeks, but she widened her eyes in an appearance of guileless innocence.

"Yes, she has," came his flat reply, and her clue that her guise had failed miserably. "Oh, never fear, I shan't tax her for it, but I know Mama rather too well. I suppose she said I was the most perfect son in the land, too."

"Oh, not perfect, my lord," said Claire with a smile, realising he was sharper than she'd given him credit for, and deciding it best to abandon pretence. "But she does rather like you. Do you still love that female?" Silently, she cursed herself for asking so personal a question. Why should she care if he was still in love with the lady?

"No, I don't. It was long ago, and I only thought myself in love with her. In fact, I'm happily rid of her. Saved from a fate worse than death, you might say. Besides, I had no need of an heir then."

"But still you might have found a lady you could like." The words were out before she could stop them.

His brows furrowed, and after a moment, he asked, "Who is to say I cannot like you?"

"I only feel it so, my lord. You scarcely kissed me at the church." Not that she would have wanted him to, of course.

"I feared you'd swoon if I did. A rather embarrassing predicament, don't you suppose, to have my wife fainting at my first touch?" He grinned sardonically, and before she knew what he was about, he had closed the space between them, and taken both her hands in his. "If you desire me to rectify my oversight, I daresay I'd be delighted to."

Claire gaped at him and pulled back, eyes wide, cheeks hot. His proximity put her entirely out of countenance. "I—I wasn't asking for a kiss, my lord!" she sputtered, flustered. "I merely thought I had given you a disgust of myself."

"Claire," he murmured, gazing into her eyes, and lifting a hand to brush a stray tendril from her face, "your charms are the last I'd take in disgust."

'Twas another reminder that he'd married her for her beauty alone. His thumb ran softly from earlobe to chin, burning a trail along her jawline. Claire lowered her lashes, hoping to hide the fact that she found the sensation all too pleasurable. Then he was gone, returning to the other seat with the same swift grace as before.

It took her a second to marshal her thoughts, though one question reigned supreme: if he hadn't taken her in disgust, why had he run off to the country? Hot on the heels of that, rose up another puzzle. "My lord, if the lady we spoke of earlier merely wanted your money, then pray tell why you would deny her and accept me, as I am truly no better."

His gaze flicked across the space separating them. "I know where I stand with you. You've made no pretence of affection; indeed, quite the opposite. Your honesty is refreshing, and I find it far less tedious than playing silly games of feigned love for gains too delicate to mention."

She nodded, seeing why he would think that way. He'd been perfectly frank with her since their dance at Almack's, not offering the slightest pretence that he cared for her. And she agreed that a marriage based on a cold contract would be better than one made of lies. She studied him covertly until his gaze met hers. Straightening, she turned her attention to the scene beyond her window.

They were on the Dover Road now, yet were still surrounded by an inordinate amount of humanity. "My lord, why are all these people with us?" she asked.

"My servants need to return to my estate also, as my town house will now be closed for some time. I decided the ones who weren't needed there should travel with us. I trust you have no objections?"

"I can't think why I would." Her gaze returned to the window. She recalled her family's trip from Sussex to London; they'd sent their servants ahead. No procession of liveried outriders had escorted them. It must be owing to Nicolas's consequence, and position in Society, which would also explain why his servants carried pistols at their sides.

CLAIRE NERVOUSLY PACED her bedchamber, her gaze skittering over the pleasing pink-and-white decor. They'd arrived at Kenwood Park at midafternoon. She'd met the servants, and after taking tea, had received a brief tour of the main rooms. Although huge, the Tudor-style house exuded an aura of warmth and welcome. The servants, happy and at ease, apparently performed their jobs well. The beeswax shine on the furniture was a wonder to behold, and the meal served them at dinner might have graced the Prince Regent's table.

It came as a pleasant surprise to discover that Nicolas had shunned the main dining room in favour of the smaller breakfast parlour. The servants had created a soft, romantic atmosphere with candles, freshly cut roses and the finest silver dinnerware. 'Twas a scene fit for new lovers, but Claire made sure it wasn't at all appropriate. Romance didn't figure in her and Nicolas's contract. But Nicolas had seemed in a relaxed, congenial mood, and the meal had passed tolerably well.

Now she awaited her husband, wondering if perhaps, just perhaps, he might allow her to retire alone tonight. A hopeless wish, to be sure. Surely he would come. 'Twas why he'd married her, after all. He needed an heir, and she had sealed their bargain with her vows.

She crossed her arms in front of her, feeling decidedly unclad. That silly maid had insisted on dressing her in the most revealing of costumes, a white diaphanous gown which was a horrid affront to Claire's modesty. Emma had departed, rapturously extolling her mistress's beauty. One brief glance in the full-length mirror had sent Claire rushing to the wardrobe and her worn, yet serviceable and enveloping, robe.

Her fingers curled into her palms, the nails biting hard into her tender flesh. She could scarcely entertain the thought of what would come. It was too awful to think of his kissing her, of his hands actually touching her flesh. To think of . . .

A strangled sound erupted from her throat, and she whirled about to pace to the other end of the room. Perhaps she should extinguish the candles and get into bed. Then, at least, he wouldn't be able to see how very distraught she was. And it would be much easier to endure if they were shrouded in darkness.

Would that action expose her cowardice, or worse yet, make her appear too eager? She grimaced with indecision. Why, oh why, could she not control these turbulent thoughts and summon her courage to face with dignity the event to come? *Calm yourself, Claire Elizabeth,* she admonished. *This is your duty, and whether or not you like it, you shall perform it. You haven't any choice.*

The connecting door opened. Her nerves threatened to snap, and she whirled round, eyes wide, her breath caught in her throat. Instinctively, she clutched her robe closer and regarded her husband in silent, dubious dread.

His hair, a trifle mussed, looked as if he'd drawn his fingers through it repeatedly. One curly lock slanted across his forehead, falling just above straight brows. Black lashes made a startling contrast to silver grey eyes; lean cheeks and a strong jaw gave way to generously curved lips. Clad in a brocade dressing-gown, calves and feet bare, he looked wonderfully handsome and exceedingly forbidding.

An assessing grey gaze swept her from head to foot, and returned to her face. Muttering softly beneath his breath, he turned, saying, ''I'll be back in a moment.''

Claire's breath rushed out in a whoosh. The connecting door stood ajar, and she stared at it, praying for composure. That cold regard still had the power to unnerve her.

He was back in an instant, bearing a decanter of brandy and two glasses. He measured the liquor, handing her a portion and bidding her to sit. Gingerly, she backed into a chair, unable to take her eyes from him.

He took a chair opposite, lowering his length in one lithe, graceful movement, stretching his legs before him. In that moment, Claire despised him for all his self-assurance, his confidence and ease, for the fact that he was her husband and had the right to impose himself upon her.

"Drink your brandy, Claire," Nicolas said, sipping his own. Egad, the woman was terrified! God grant him patience with her virginal fears! She clutched at her horrid robe as if she faced rape.

Would she have shown this fright were Robert West her husband? He doubted it, and the knowledge chilled his blood. He tossed back his brandy and set the glass aside. He couldn't make love to her with the spectre of Robert West looming between them. 'Twould be hell waiting until she gave herself freely, but he wouldn't take her until she could.

He sighed. "The intimacy between a man and his wife can be pleasurable, Claire," he said softly. "Certainly I will not force myself upon you, though I must insist you allow yourself to become accustomed to my presence—and my touch." His gaze slid from her lustrous, unbound locks to the feminine curves lurking beneath the hideous robe. "I'll try my best to be patient."

"That puts me at my ease," Claire said, a tinge of waspishness in her voice. Allow herself to become accustomed to his touch? Was that possible? "Pray, just how much patience might I expect, my lord?"

"Not enough to suit you, I'm sure," came his dry answer. He stood, flexing his shoulders and rubbing a hand along the back of his neck. His robe lifted with the movement, revealing a strong and shapely calf, covered with fine dark hairs. Claire endeavoured to ignore the handsome sight.

He studied her for some moments. "I can only promise to proceed as slowly and carefully as I am able to in the hopes that one day you'll allow me the freedom of my rightful place." A long, considering pause punctuated his words. "Come to me, Claire."

She flinched at the quiet command. For some reason, she thought he'd simply leave the room, without any further ado. Her sudden flare of relief died instantly. She might have known he wouldn't. Rising slowly from her chair, her spine stiff and straight, she walked to him and waited with wary expectancy.

Fright and dislike oozed from every line of her rigid pose. Nicolas was at a loss how best to proceed with this wife who clearly despised him and shrank from his touch. Robert West's words flashed into his mind. *"Rather galling to know, isn't it, that your wife is in love with another man?"* Damn and blast, yes, it was galling!

He wanted to curse aloud and stalk from the room, but for the sake of an heir, he stayed his ground. He wouldn't, couldn't, have patience with her shrinking ways forever. Damn, knowing he wouldn't bed her tonight was torture enough!

"Kiss me."

Her head snapped up. "Excuse me?"

He sighed and tried again. "Have you ever been kissed by a man, Claire?"

Her eyes flashed green fire. "No, my lord. If I didn't kiss Robert West, you might be sure I've never kissed another."

"Indeed" was his flat reply, though he gleaned a certain satisfaction from knowing he would have what West hadn't. "Then tonight you shall." He wanted to sweep her into his arms and force his lips upon her, but didn't doubt she'd swoon. Best let her lead. "Come closer and kiss me."

She regarded him with uncertainty, but took a pace forward. Lifting her mouth, she planted a quick peck on his cheek.

Nicolas gaped at her for one stupefied second. He swallowed. What had he expected? She was, without a doubt, a complete innocent. He clamped an urgent hand on his frustration. "On the lips, Claire," he said slowly, in strained tones. "Let me show you."

His hand glided beneath the silky strands of her hair to the nape of her neck. He tilted her head, and brought his down ever so carefully, his gaze fused with hers. His thumb caressed the erratic pulse thumping in her throat. She was as frightened as a rabbit caught in a snare. He wondered that he didn't just leave the room and put her out of her panic.

The delightful proximity of her sweet mouth stayed him, and he took her lips in a tender, yet lingering kiss. Though he sensed her alarm and lack of response, he delighted in tasting her lush softness. He lifted his head after a few moments, all frustration deserting him.

Her face wore a considering expression, and he was emboldened to murmur, "There now, was that so bad?"

Claire studied him with some bewilderment. Alarm and panic had flown, leaving her feeling soft and trembly. It wasn't really so awful as she'd imagined. Indeed, it had been quite ... nice. She couldn't confess that, though, so ventured a different reply. "Your lips are warm, my lord."

A strangled gulp, sounding much like amused astonishment, erupted from his throat. "Did you expect otherwise?" he queried. "I do believe most parts of the human body remain at a constant temperature under normal circumstances."

She lowered her head, blushing. She had thought his lips would be as cold as his icy eyes, like a frozen winter pond. A finger beneath her chin lifted her face to his. For a moment, she thought he would kiss her again, and a tiny tremor of excitement rippled through her. But he merely considered her, his eyes having lost their iciness.

"Now," he said quietly, "there are two further things I wish from you tonight. First, I wish you to call me Nicolas, as you've been 'my lording' me all day."

"Yes, my lord," she said, tilting her chin higher.

"Nicolas," he said, his eyes locking with hers in a silent, yet firm, command.

She stared long into those grey depths, and gave an infinitesimal shrug. "Nicolas."

"And second, I want you to take off that dreadful robe and consign it to the rubbish heap."

Nicolas was quite unprepared for the panic which flashed through her eyes. As if by instinct, she clutched at the robe with both hands, holding it protectively about her.

"Right now, my lor ... Nicolas?" she whispered, her eyes wide.

"Yes, now. I trust you have something on beneath it?"

Would he make her part with it if she said no? Claire couldn't bring herself to speak the lie, in case he did. Alarm lent warmth to her cheeks. "Yes, but, my ...

Nicolas, it is the most horribly revealing thing, and I shall be mortified should you see me in it!''

''Did your mother teach you nothing? Physical intimacy often requires not a stitch of clothing. Be assured, wife, I shall see you in less than that 'ere long.''

Claire castigated herself for a missish gudgeon, chagrined that her dignity could so have fled her. He would want to see what he'd purchased, of course. She drew herself up to her full height, and commanded her fingers to loose their death grip. ''Yes, my mother warned me what to expect. However, it seemed easier to hear of it than to perform it.''

Drawing the robe off her shoulders, she let it drop to the floor. Head held high, she refused to look at him. Still, it was difficult to keep her breath steady as she awaited his reaction. He lifted a tentative hand, and she froze. Slowly he caressed the length of her side from breast to hip. Her flesh tingled where his fingers trailed, and she marvelled at the pleasurable sensation they left in their place.

Nicolas had never seen a more beautiful sight. Claire's scanty nightgown displayed her charms most effectively, and he rather thought it might have been more conducive to his peace of mind had she kept the blasted robe on. He stepped back, his hand dropping to his side.

''You are indeed wondrously made,'' he breathed. His voice sounded raw, and he knew another moment of this awesome sight would undo his resolve. His gaze moved to hers, and he said unsteadily, ''I bid you goodnight, wife.''

He turned away, rapidly closing the distance between himself and the connecting door. He was through it in an instant, the soft click of the latch following a mere instant later.

Claire, bewildered, stared after him. She moved slowly about the room, extinguishing the candles. Slipping between the lavender-scented sheets, she stared at the darkened silk hangings draping her bed. One finger lightly traced her lips.

His kiss wasn't at all what she'd feared. Smooth lips, almost soft, had held a hint of mastery and confidence she somehow found as appealing as it was unnerving. His face danced before her. She recalled his slender fingers sliding through her hair, his thumb gently caressing her throbbing pulse. Her heart performed an erratic flip-flop, and she sighed.

She'd given him cause for impatience, yet he'd let her be. Her knowledge of his character hadn't prepared her for such magnanimity. He'd chosen her from the Marriage Mart, as coldly calculating as if she'd been a prize brood mare. He'd paid the price, so why hadn't he demanded she pay hers?

She wondered if Robert would have shown the same generosity, and why she hadn't thought of him until now. Would his kiss have inspired these strange sensations inside her? Surely. One man's kiss, after all, couldn't be so different from another's.

She conjured up Robert's laughing blue eyes, and with a frown, rolled over on her bed. Robert's kiss would have been much nicer. And she wouldn't have wanted him to leave.

The Earl of Kenton might take her body, but he could never take her heart.

NICOLAS SPRAWLED atop his bed. A dive in the cool waters of the Strait would be beneficial to his peace, if not his health. That green-eyed beauty had bewitched him.

And she as frightened as a bunny! She surely despised him even more than he had thought.

"All your riches won't purchase her love," West's voice taunted. He didn't want her love ... but he didn't want her hate, either. What did he want? Her regard, her respect? Yes, but he needed an heir, and begetting him, it seemed, wouldn't be so simple as he'd imagined. He couldn't take a woman who loathed his very touch.

He'd have to make her want him, and if he could oust Robert West from her thoughts at the same time, so much the better. He'd have to woo her gently, he decided, and with as much haste as was seemly.

CHAPTER SEVEN

A SCRATCHING AT HER DOOR wakened Claire. A mob-capped maid entered, bearing a tray.

"Good morning, m'lady," she said shyly. "Mrs. Trumble said as how she forgot to ask if you liked your chocolate in bed. She had me bring it just in case, so as not to displease your ladyship."

"Thank you," murmured Claire, thinking the idea sounded delightful. She'd never taken her chocolate in bed. Being a countess did have its advantages. She sat up, pulling the blankets with her, and smiled, asking the maid her name.

"My name be Maggie, your ladyship," the girl answered, bobbing a curtsy.

Her new title still sounded strange. Claire was entirely unused to the bobs, curtsies, and bows, the *miladys* and *your ladyships*. She wondered if she would become accustomed eventually, or continue to find them as frustrating as Fanny did.

"What time is it?" she asked Maggie. Upon receiving the answer of ten o'clock, she added, "And his lordship...has he breakfasted yet?"

"Oh, yes, mum. At least two hours ago, but he said as we weren't to disturb you. If it pleases your ladyship, I'll send Emma to help you dress. His lordship said as how he'd await your convenience in the study, as he'd be pleased to give you a tour of the house this morning."

"Thank you, Maggie. I shall be ready to dress in twenty minutes." Maggie left the room with a final bob. Claire followed her retreat with a thoughtful gaze. Normally, the chore of showing the house was reserved for the housekeeper. Why should Nicolas choose to take on the task?

Claire had hoped she wouldn't see him until dinner. True, they were newlyweds, but she wished they could escape doing the pretty. She sipped her chocolate, mulling over the previous evening.

Perhaps she had behaved rather missishly. But how else might she have responded to the idea of being intimate with her husband? She knew so very little of him. Still, she was no longer a child. It behooved her to act as the woman she was. And, she was forced to admit, he wasn't unattractive.

AFTER BREAKFAST, Claire tapped on the study door. Nicolas's low, well-modulated voice bade her enter, and she turned the knob, wishing she might have delayed this moment. Facing her husband after last night wasn't in the least comfortable.

He sat behind a large desk. As she shut the door, he rose, coming round to lounge against the polished oak. He was casually dressed, his buckskin breeches tucked into polished Hessians. His white linen shirt, sleeves rolled to the elbows, had several buttons loosed, displaying a light curling of hairs on his chest. He looked more handsome and virile than she cared to admit.

"Good morning," she said, hoping her tone sounded as cool and impersonal as she intended.

"Good morning. I trust you slept well?" Nicolas hoped she'd slept better than he, for his night had been hellish. Warring with his manly urges had been difficult enough; but the question of how he might bring her to him, soft and willing, had nagged at him constantly.

Surely he could stamp West from her mind, he'd reasoned, but now an uneasiness assailed him. What if he couldn't? Would anything he tried succeed? Would she ever forget that rogue and desire her husband? And dammit! Why should he be obliged to try? She was his wife; he shouldn't have to manoeuvre for her favours.

But she was so beautiful. Her pale blue morning gown and the matching ribbon in her hair made her a delightful picture. Her green eyes were tilted up at him, expressing a polite, yet cool, enquiry. He realised he'd been staring, and wondered if his face reflected his inner battle. Well, he decided, his mission must begin, and he could but try to wrest her affections from West.

He smiled, moving forward to take both her hands in his. He lightly kissed the fingers of each. His gaze caressed her face throughout. "You look lovely today, lady wife."

"Thank you," murmured Claire. What queer start had he taken? Her cold, aloof husband kissing her fingers? She didn't want to acknowledge the pleasant fluttering his action provoked. But she couldn't tear her gaze away from his lips, nor help thinking that only last night, they'd taken hers in a kiss softer and warmer than she'd thought a kiss from him might be.

His gaze, she finally realised, was fixed on her, and she quickly looked away. *Gad, Claire,* she admonished herself, *you needn't ogle quite so openly!* She rushed into speech, hoping to hide her confusion. "You wanted to show me the house, my lord?"

"Yes."

His smile was nice, quite nice. More than that, it was...attractive. The thought of kissing him again swept over her like a sudden deluge. She concentrated on the toes of her slippers, her body growing warm. Whatever was she thinking? A trifle breathless, she asked, "Are you ready, or should I return later?"

"I'm ready. Come." Instead of offering his arm, he took her hand in a gentle, but firm, clasp.

Claire gave a nervous jump, so startling was the contact. She peeked up at him, but his lashes shuttered the expression in his eyes. What was he thinking? He looked almost grim. Her hand rested in his, though she didn't dare to curl her fingers round his palm. Robert had held her hand several times, but somehow the pressure of his palm against hers had never been so unnerving. Holding Nicolas's hand had an intimate quality Robert's clasp had lacked.

Nicolas drew her from the study and into the main hallway. He liked the feel of her hand in his. Her soft skin and delicate bones sharpened his awareness of how appealingly feminine she was. He twined his little finger round hers, knowing she'd twitch again, which she did. Gad, he wished she didn't hate him so! Did his heir stand a chance of being conceived?

He'd seen Claire staring at his lips, and had taken heart, believing, hoping, wishing, praying that perhaps, just perhaps, she'd liked his kiss. But she was still as nervous as a doe in hunting season—and he was hunting, he made no doubt. His mouth curled in a sardonic smile.

He opened a door and ushered her through it, the movement necessitating the release of her hand. He didn't doubt her thankfulness; she immediately clasped her fingers together before her. "This is the music room, as you've no doubt concluded. Do you play any of these pieces?"

"I play the harp," Claire answered, walking forward to assess that instrument. Evidently in excellent repair, the piece was of a quality high above the battered one her parents kept. She ran her fingertips across the strings. A soft melody rippled forth and her lips lifted. She looked across at Nicolas. "It's a very beautiful instrument, my lord. Do you play?"

"Not the harp, but I'm passable on the pianoforte. I haven't a notion why the rest are kept. Decoration, I suppose. I hope you feel free to use them anytime."

"Thank you, I shall," Claire returned with a quick smile.

"Shall we continue our tour?" he asked, this time offering his arm.

Claire nodded, refusing the urge to ignore his arm proffered in escort. Such churlishness sat ill with her, even if his proximity was unnerving. Besides, taking his arm was much easier than holding his hand. He would have no opportunity to curl his little finger round hers, and thus throw her out of countenance. However, the strength of his arm and the warmth of his skin penetrating white linen did little for her peace of mind. She wondered if she'd feel less intimidated and more inclined towards friendliness were he more approachable.

The morning passed speedily. Nicolas was kind and pleasing; though, as ever, a hint of restraint coloured his manner. That difference between him and Robert was markedly clear. Robert could never be described as restrained. Claire pondered this a moment, and was shocked to realise that Robert's lack of reserve had made her somewhat uneasy. Of course, she reasoned quickly, Nicolas's tendency in the opposite direction could be no better. But why, then, did she appreciate it more? Why did she find it almost reassuring?

"And now for the picture gallery," Nicolas said, interrupting her musings. "I promise this will end our tour."

Claire's lips twitched. Indeed, it had seemed monstrous long, so large was the house. The thought of lunch beckoned, but the portraits of Nicolas's ancestors enticed, and her mind soon deserted the thought of food.

"The first Earl of Kenton," Nicolas said, pointing to the likeness of a man looking more like a buccaneer than a noble lord. "His name was Dominic Shea. He won accolade—and his title—from the King for patrolling the coasts hereabouts, and . . . well, for more or less keeping the area free of smugglers." He lifted his fist, clearing his throat.

That obviously wasn't an end of the story. "And . . . ?" Claire prompted, intrigued.

"And," said Nicolas with a hint of a smile, "in my own humble opinion, he was the worst pirate of the lot." He pointed to the painting of a lovely girl with large, solemn dark eyes. "The first Countess of Kenton. He kidnapped her from an Italian merchantman, along with the rest of the goods on board."

"Poor girl," Claire cried, shocked at the first earl's heartlessness and pitying the young lady who stared so soberly from the canvas. "She must have been terribly unhappy."

"For a while I believe she was. But Mama told me that she and Dominic fell in love and enjoyed a blissful union. It seems she had a settling effect on him, and he left his . . . *pirating*—albeit in the name of the King—and gave himself over to a life befitting an earl." He gestured at the next picture. "Thus they produced Fane, their son and heir to the title."

Slowly, they moved along the gallery, Nicolas regaling Claire with tales of each successor to the line. "There's always been one son born of each union," he explained. "A blessing indeed; however, it leaves no heir to the title should that son die without issue. Fortunately, such tragedy hasn't yet occurred."

And she was beside him, thought Claire, for the sole purpose of seeing it did not. 'Twas rather jolting to realise her grandson would join the others in due time. Would her great-grandson say to his new wife, as he waved a hand towards her portrait, "This is Claire, the fifth Countess of Kenton, bought by Nicolas to secure his line. Mama tells me she wasn't the happiest of brides, but..." Would she, like the Italian girl, come to love her husband? And he her? She glanced across at Nicolas. No, it truly wasn't possible.

"You can see why," Nicolas said, his low voice breaking through her thought, "I so desire an heir. I'd feel a gross failure to my ancestors did I die without succession. They worked long and hard to establish the line of Kenton and all that is bequeathed with that title: the estate, the farms...and all else."

Claire gave a tiny nod of acknowledgement. Yes, she could see, but she heartily wished she hadn't been chosen as the one to produce that successor. She stopped before the next portrait, surveying the handsome lord depicted therein.

"That's my father," Nicolas said quietly from behind her. Something in his voice captured her attention. A certain note of...what? Pride? Sadness?

"You resemble him," she commented. The same piercing grey eyes watched her from the canvas. "Do you miss him?"

"Very much. He was killed in a hunting accident, and I was in no wise ready to step into his shoes and assume responsibility for the family."

Claire turned to him, noting the brief clouding of his eyes. A pang of pity for him assailed her. The weight of duty Nicolas had shouldered must have been onerous. She had an idea how heavy such a burden could be. He didn't seem inclined to elaborate any further, so she stepped to the next portrait. "Ah, and here is Fanny. She's very pretty, don't you think?"

He smiled. "Yes, Mama was considered quite the diamond in her day."

Claire nodded absently, her attention captured by the likeness of her husband.

"That was painted when I reached my majority," Nicolas explained. "Mama insisted upon engaging Sir Thomas Lawrence."

"He's very talented," Claire acknowledged. She studied the portrait closely, noting Nicolas's laughing eyes and carefree grin. He had a devil-may-care handsomeness, with his dark curly locks in disorder. She looked at Nicolas, comparing him with his younger self.

"Time has a way of changing one's attitude," he said with a shrug, and she suspected he knew her thoughts.

"What took that look of merry devilment from your face?"

Another shrug. "Maturity, responsibility, disillusionment, I suppose."

Claire took another good look at the younger Nicolas, pondering what it might have been like to meet *that* man.

"As you know, likenesses of my sisters, Letty and Belle, are hung in the drawing room," Nicolas said.

Claire nodded, recalling the pretty dark-haired girls in the portraits. "And when shall I meet them? I had hoped to do so at the wedding, but your mother said they were both increasing. That must be exciting for you. I know Fanny is in alt."

"I daresay we'll see them after the babes are born." A contemplative expression flitted across his face. "And yes, I suppose it is rather exciting, even if Letty already has one child." He chuckled. "I simply can't imagine Belle having a babe. She's quite a flighty little thing."

"But you said the same of your mama, and though perhaps she is, I still think she has good sense and a deeper understanding than one would first expect."

"You like my mother?"

"Very much," she replied with a nod.

"She likes you as well," he said. "She told me I couldn't have done better for myself."

"Kind of her to say so," Claire acknowledged, inclining her head. She wondered if Nicolas agreed, but didn't dare to ask.

"If you'd like, we might have lunch, and tour the grounds later, if you wish."

"That would be fine," she responded, taking the arm he offered.

At lunch, during which she noted that he had ordered her place set to his immediate right, she mused, "The house is so very large, I wonder you use half of it."

"I'm sure we don't. However, when we were growing up, it was filled. My sisters and I, our parents, nannies, governesses, tutors: it was a much busier place then. I sometimes find the lack of activity onerous, after having known busier days. I should like to fill the rooms with the laughter of children. Do you like children, Claire?"

She considered a moment, imagining the vast rooms and hallways ringing with the sounds of pattering feet and shrill little voices. The thought warmed her. "Yes, I rather think I do."

He smiled and reached across to her, his fingers gently caressing the back of her hand. "I rather think I should have asked you that before proposing. I'm happy to hear your affirmation, though." He cocked an eyebrow. "Should you like to get started on that endeavour?"

She blushed, shyness and confusion overtaking her. Her gaze fell to her hand, and she watched his fingertips smooth along it, wondering at the strange sensations which fluttered within her at his touch.

"My lord," she ventured after some moments, "I am your wife, and as such, will do my best to fulfil my obligations to you. I apologize for my missishness last night, and thank you kindly for your understanding. I shall try harder to please you."

Nicolas's fingers lifted abruptly and he sat back on his chair, crossing his arms before him. Were he a cad, he'd take her at her word right now, and blast lunch, the servants and the remainder of the afternoon. But he wasn't a cad, and it sat ill with him that she should see their lovemaking as a sacrifice, a duty she must submit to.

"Claire," he finally responded, "your intentions are noble, I'm assured. However, I don't find the thought of making love to a martyr all that stimulating."

Anger spat from her eyes. She regarded him with silent mutiny. "You've paid for your heir, my lord," she said in cool and dignified tones. "'Twould be dishonourable of me should I fail to keep my end of our bargain."

"Indeed," he said dryly. "Your sense of duty is most worthy. How is your soup?"

STROLLING ABOUT the fragrant, manicured gardens soothed Claire's nerves. The warmth of the day and the fresh summer scents were relaxing reminders of how well she loved the country life. Her hand resting in the crook of her husband's arm, she listened to him explain the history of his home, from the first Earl of Kenton, to himself. She found his discourse fascinating, and sensed his deep love for his heritage.

The third earl, keeping to the original Tudor style, had added two wings to the house and created the maze in the centre of the garden. Fanny, she learned, was responsible for the rosebushes which grew in profusion, surrounding small arbours containing whitewashed benches and an occasional fountain.

Outside the kitchen, a small patch of ground was set aside for a herb garden—the credit for which belonged to Nicolas's grandmother. Most of it was neglected and overrun with weeds. Herbs being one of Claire's passions, she decided to return it to life at the first opportunity. Keeping her hands occupied would surely ease the pangs of settling into her new home.

"Do you ride, Claire?" Nicolas asked upon their return to the courtyard. He pointed to the long low building of the stables. "We can look at the horses if you'd like."

Claire's heart lifted, and she smiled. "Oh, yes, I should like that, Nicolas. I love to ride."

A look akin to pleasure crossed his face, and his eyes lighted. "I'm pleased to hear you say so. I have a mare I thought might be perfect for you. I hope she meets with your approval, but of course, you may choose as you wish."

Nicolas introduced her to Sundance, a trim-lined sorrel with a flaxen mane and tail. Claire could well imagine how the sun would dance off her burnished coat, highlighting her soft copper-and-blond hide.

"Oh, Nicolas, she's a beauty," Claire purred, smoothing her hand over the mare's velvety muzzle and along her jaw. Perhaps life at Kenwood Park wouldn't be as onerous as she feared. She gave Nicolas a bright smile. "Thank you."

Nicolas stepped closer, lifting a finger. For a startled second, Claire thought he might touch her bottom lip, but he checked, and instead captured a stray hair and tucked it behind her ear. The pad of his finger lingered in that vulnerable hollow behind her lobe, before his hand fell to his side.

"No need." His voice was a caress, scarcely louder than a whisper. He cleared his throat. "I hope you enjoy her. Your being new to the district, Claire, it would be best if you would ride out with either me or a groom until you become more familiar with the territory."

"Of course. I shouldn't like to distress you by becoming lost."

"Indeed. Shall we continue indoors? There's more I'd like to show you."

With a final pat to the mare's satiny neck, Claire took her husband's arm. He escorted her back into the sunshine, past the gardens and green to a small knoll overlooking an orchard. Explaining the origin of the orchard, he turned her about to view the scene from whence they'd come. The house and grounds spread before them in picturesque display, engendering a sense of peace and serenity Claire had never experienced.

"Oh, it is lovely," she breathed.

"You can see why I so desire to have a son to carry on." He took her hand, smoothing his thumb across her palm. "Claire, should I die before I see my son born, you will remember to teach him all I've told you today?"

"Whyever should you die before he is born?"

He shrugged, his eyes evading her searching look. "A man never knows from one day to the next."

"Please, don't speak of such things as death and dying! It makes me feel oddly deflated, and the day is so perfect, I should like to enjoy it to the fullest." Why should the thought of him dead fill her with such plaguey feelings?

Nicolas bowed slightly in her direction. "My apologies, lady wife. I suppose once I start talking of all I love, I grow somewhat fearful lest I'm not able to teach my son as my father taught me."

"You loved your father?" Claire thought how she loved Sir Percival, and how affected she would be by his demise. She instantly dismissed the unpleasant idea.

"Very much. Though we had governesses and nannies and tutors, my parents were ever present to tend to our needs. My father taught me to ride and hunt, much to Mama's dismay." He chuckled. "Mama could never understand the thrill of bagging a pheasant or skinning a deer."

Despite herself, Claire shuddered. "And will you teach our son these things?"

He squeezed her hand. "If I'm here, my lady, I surely shall. But I grow morbid again. Come, I have one more thing to show you." He turned her again, this time towards the sparkling blue waters which crested a shimmering border about his lands. He led her down the knoll towards the rippling expanse. "The Strait of Dover. From this point, as we are some few miles north of Dover, Calais is no more than a twenty-five-mile trip. A strong man in a rowboat, if the currents are with him, can make the journey in six to eight hours.''

Claire gazed across the sun-kissed water, imagining rowing across to an unseen shore. ''Have you done so, my lord? Rowed across, I mean.''

''Yes, and a more onerous task I cannot imagine.''

''But surely not with the war being fought?'' she asked.

Nicolas chuckled. ''A man doesn't row to France nowadays unless he has to.''

Claire glanced at him, wondering at the cryptic remark. She hadn't a chance to question it.

''You must never come to the beach alone, Claire, especially at night,'' he said. ''We live in prime smuggling territory, and they're an ugly lot. Though I daresay none of them use this beach, I want your assurance that you shan't come here.''

''Of course,'' she agreed. She had no desire to be near the men she'd heard such awful tales about. However, the Strait looked so pretty during the day, she didn't wonder that it would be beautiful by night. ''But perhaps, Nicolas, you could bring me down here? I should truly love to behold its splendours by the light of the moon.''

''Perhaps,'' he assented. ''We'll see.''

AT BEDTIME, Claire didn't fuss when Emma laid out a shimmery pink confection no less revealing than the previous night's costume. She spared a thought for how these flimsy garments had found their way into her wardrobe, making no doubt Fanny and her mother were responsible. The two ladies had gone shopping alone one day and returned giggling like schoolgirls. Claire wasn't sure she appreciated their thoughtfulness one whit.

However, she had no fear that Nicolas wouldn't keep to his own chambers tonight. He'd escorted her to her door, and wished her pleasant dreams. She took that as a dismissal, and wondered that he didn't push the matter of an heir. He confused her, this husband. He'd been ever so nice, touching her gently on the hand, running his fingers over hers. She remembered thinking on the eve of her wedding that surely Nicolas would be a cold and aloof mate, distant and uncaring. But today he'd shown himself attentive and solicitous... even to the point of kindness.

But he hadn't kissed her, which bothered her. She couldn't understand why she would want him to, why she had enjoyed his kiss, and why she hadn't once thought of Robert during the day. Strange, but she'd never waited in expectation of Robert's kiss. She hadn't really thought about it. And perhaps it wasn't honourable of her to think it of the man she loved, but even Robert hadn't shown her the attention and courtesy Nicolas had this day.

She went to the window, lifting back the curtain. A figure paced the beach. Nicolas? Why was he down there, especially when he had expressly forbidden her to go? He moved behind a rock and disappeared. She sat for a long time, watching, but he didn't appear again. Then she heard a soft whirring noise and his voice—coming from his chamber.

She flicked back the curtain and, quiet as a mouse, slipped into bed. How had he gained his room without appearing again? She hadn't missed him, that she knew. She hadn't once taken her eyes from the place. However had he done that?

CHAPTER EIGHT

ANOTHER NIGHT PASSED, and no sign of West. How did he fare? Nicolas couldn't dismiss a feeling of unease at the thought of never seeing the man again. Cautioning himself that it had only been two days did nothing to relieve his distress.

Nicolas dismissed Forsythe, his valet, with a wave of his hand, and sprawled fully clothed upon his bed. Folding his hands behind his head, he stared at the ceiling. He knew he shouldn't be getting into a pucker so soon, but the nagging uneasiness persisted. The fear that he wouldn't be alive to raise his son, or tend his wife, gnawed at him. And blast, but he hadn't even *begun* to create an heir!

He'd thought the process of begetting a son would be a simple task, and found it damned inconvenient that things weren't proceeding according to plan. Oh, he had no doubt Claire would now take her rightful place in his life. The temptation to go to her tugged against his sure knowledge that she'd hate every moment of their union. Yes, she would submit to her duty, but his better nature demanded he regard her feelings and not force himself upon her.

He stirred restlessly upon the bed, thinking the whole matter the very deuce of a coil. He wanted an heir, but he also wanted Claire, every beautiful curve of her, and she loved the only man who could possibly save his life. Devil take it! He wanted her to come willingly, but egad, he didn't have the patience of a saint!

He swung his legs over the side of the bed and walked to his wardrobe. Wrenching it open, he snatched up his greatcoat and slung it over his shoulders. Two minutes later, he strode into the stables, barking at his groom to saddle his bay.

"I'm off to Dover, John," he explained more gently, seeking to quell his bad humour. "I feel in need of some good, strong ale."

"You thinkin' of goin' alone?" John grunted, swinging the saddle onto the bay's back.

John, one of Nicolas's few well-trusted servants, knew of his master's secret doings, and of the danger to his life. Nicolas acknowledged the logic of not going alone. "Perhaps you should accompany me."

"And are a man and his master to take drink together in a common taproom? I think not. Either give me some of your fancy togs, or I'll give you some of mine." John edged the bit between the stallion's teeth, casting Nicolas a sidelong glance.

Nicolas sighed, shrugging. "Very well, I shall impersonate your undergroom this night. Bring me a hat and coat. I rather think I can keep my breeches and shirt."

John nodded, whisking off to fetch the needed clothing. Twenty minutes of hard riding by the light of a full moon saw them alighting before one of Dover's less frequented inns. Nicolas had no desire to be recognized as the lord of Kenwood Park in his present state of dress.

The taproom hummed with a scruffy assortment of customers. The poor lighting gave Nicolas cause for thanks, but still he pulled his hat lower over his forehead, and directed John to a small table near the back corner. Nicolas rather thought they were lucky to find it, so full was the taproom with bawdy riff-raff. The two men arguing at the table behind him were decidedly rough-looking. He would certainly not grace this establishment with his presence again.

"You order the ale, John," he said, drawing some coins from his pocket and placing them on the rough-hewn table. He knew his cultivated speech would be remarked upon in an instant among this crop of undesirables.

A saucy serving wench flounced to their table, assessing them with a practised eye. John immediately bade her bring two ales. The girl sniffed and turned on her heel, swinging her hips in an exaggerated fashion back to the tap. Minutes later, she set two mugs of frothy brew before them, and deftly caught the coin John flipped her.

Nicolas sat back, taking a long pull of the ale. The men behind him argued louder now, partly, he assumed, to be heard above the din, and partly because they'd each had their share of drink. More bored than curious, Nicolas turned his ear to their conversation. He heard his name mentioned and a chill like an icy finger ran up his spine.

"A proper lord," one said, "and livin' close enough to make the trip to France in a single night."

"But a *lord*," replied the other. "Don't want to be messin' with that unless we're dead certain. 'Sides, heard somewheres as how he just got hisself buckled. Ain't no man 'ull be taking a bride if he's cavortin' to France every night. Daresay the little wife wouldn't like that."

"Mebbe, but—"

"No buts. I ain't gonna touch no earl till I'm that certain he's our man. Too risky."

Nicolas leaned forward, cradling his half-empty glass between his palms. "John, look past me and give me a full description of those two men. I didn't observe them closely enough when we arrived.''

John lifted cautious eyes, peering past Nicolas to the two ruffians. Slowly he counted off their attributes, or lack thereof, finishing with ''Black hair, the both of 'em. Ugly.''

''We'll deal with them tonight,'' Nicolas said in a low, steely voice. He explained what he'd overheard, adding, ''I trust you have a weapon of sorts on your person.''

''Aye, that I do,'' replied John. ''As do you, I'm certain.''

''Indeed,'' drawled Nicolas, wiggling his foot. The hard steel of his knife rubbed against his shin. The blade was such a constant companion now that he rarely remarked its presence. He lifted his tankard, draining the remaining ale, his brain busy formulating a plan.

Lie in wait for them to leave the taproom? But what if they had rooms in the inn for the night? He didn't doubt he and John alone could send the devils to their Maker, given the element of surprise and a bit of good luck. The two men being deep in their cups was an added advantage. But, where might they ambush them, disarm them with nought but knives?

''M'lord, watch yer head!'' John, rising out of his chair, pushed Nicolas aside. Nicolas's chair toppled over, leaving him stranded on the floor. He barely had time to grasp the situation for a second later, a smelly brute with gin-laced breath slid on his belly beside him, obviously having come to grief with a fellow patron.

With a roar of rage, the felled man raised himself to a hands-and-knees position. His assailant was poised above him with an empty gin bottle at the ready. Nicolas rolled over and away. The rough, heavy table crashed onto its top, legs extended into the air.

A collective bellow from the bawdy patrons of the tavern rose a moment later. Tables crashed, chairs cracked and tankards clattered against the walls and floor. Bodies grappled and feinted, some meeting forcefully with the wooden planks to lunge frantically away from pounding boots.

"Damnation!" Nicolas leapt to his feet, dodging one ham-fisted blow, only to be staggered by another connecting with his lip. Warm blood oozed and trickled down his chin. John sent the first man to his knees with a punishing clout to the shoulder. Nicolas sprawled the other with a swift uppercut to the jaw.

Backing against the wall, he grasped John's arm, dragging him away from the scene of commotion. "Where did our men go? Did you see them?"

"They cleared out like boys making off with Cook's apple tarts!"

"Damn," Nicolas muttered, casting a jaundiced eye over the tangle of brawling humanity. "Blasted Bedlamites, the lot of them. Let's get out of here."

"Right with ya, m'lord. Fresh air won't go amiss."

Plowing their way through the brouhaha was no easy task. Several chins met with Nicolas's punishing right hook and John's heavy backhand. At last the door was in sight; only one swaggering lout marred the view. Nicolas and John lunged as one towards him, sending him sprawling with nothing but their collective weights aimed at his midriff. Then they sprinted out into the cool night breeze.

"Damn and double damn," Nicolas softly swore, glancing up and down the street. "You're sure you saw them leave?"

"They made for the door lickety-split the moment they saw that animal waving the gin bottle."

Nicolas gave a frustrated grunt and smote his thigh with his fist. "Hellfire and brimstone! Of all the blasted...!"

"Here, m'lord, they don't know you're their man," John offered as a placating gesture. "We won't find 'em tonight, that's sure, but that ain't to say we can't send some men round here lookin' for 'em."

Nicolas cast him a disgruntled glance. He did have the men's descriptions, and Renshaw could probably send out a small army to search for them. But that consolation didn't put his mind to rest. To have had his foe neatly in his hands, and to lose them, made his blood burn like fire. It hadn't taken them long to include him on their list of suspects, and that knowledge was like a stone in his stomach.

He swiped at the blood oozing down his chin with the back of his hand. "Let's go home, John. I'm charging you with Claire's safety. I want you to keep a constant eye on her whenever she leaves the house. I make no doubt they'll be back."

"MY LORD," said Claire the next morning at breakfast, "where did you get that cut on your lip?" The angry swelling of Nicolas's bottom lip glared across the table. A vision of him standing on the beach rose before her. Nicolas lifted a bruised and swollen hand, gingerly touching the wound in question. "And your hand!" she exclaimed. "Nicolas, have you been fighting?"

Nicolas stared at her, looking peeved. "Yes, wife," he said in clipped tones, "I have been fighting."

"But how?" Her brows drew together. "Where...? Why?"

Nicolas sighed. How could he explain his presence in a lowly tavern? That it wasn't safe for him to ride alone into Dover, thus he had to take John, borrowing his groom's clothes because a man and his master shouldn't be seen drinking together? And because he wore his groom's clothes, he'd chosen a less desirable inn in which to go unrecognized. He coughed into his hand. "It's a long tale, Claire. Suffice it to say I was in the wrong place at the wrong time."

Jewel-green eyes raked his face, filling with suspicion. "I saw you on the beach last night. Did you run against some smugglers? Nicolas, you told me it was unsafe to go down there, so why did you? And how did you get back to your room?"

Nicolas felt like an insect specimen pinned to paper. So much for a wife who kept to her own business. He studied her, his lips twitching, his tongue trying to form any of a hundred lies to appease her. "Claire," he finally said, "I'd rather you didn't worry yourself about it. An unfortunate mishap, 'tis all. Should you like to drive into Dover today... acquaint yourself with the town?"

Her lashes dropped, her chin tilted and her lips tightened. "Very well, my lord. If that is what you wish. But mayhap I should try to disguise that angry lip before we go. I daresay it wouldn't do for the Earl of Kenton to appear in public looking as if he's participated in a brawl."

Nicolas grimaced. She said the words sweetly enough, but he gained the impression she wasn't one whit pleased with his explanation and subsequent termination of the subject. "Very well, my lady," he replied. "I daresay you are correct."

A half hour later, he sat at Claire's dressing table whilst she blended some strange concoction in a small dish. He eyed the mixture with disfavour, and she gave him a wicked grin.

"Do you fear you shall be poisoned?" she asked. "'Tis nought but some healing herbs and dye mixed in a paste. I doubt it will kill you."

"I trust your skills," he hastily assured her. She'd lost her earlier tight-lipped look, and he didn't want to say anything to bring that disapproving expression back to her face.

Claire smiled. "I don't think you do. Now tilt your head so I can apply it properly."

Nicolas did as she'd bade, but still she placed a supporting finger under his chin. She dabbed her creation gently onto his lip, smoothing with light strokes. The action was tantalizingly sensual. He quite forgot the tenderness of his injury in the sudden desire to capture her finger between his teeth. Her mouth was close to his own, so very close he would have to but lean forward an inch to claim its softness....

Claire saw his heavy-lidded appraisal of her mouth. His breath fanned her cheek, swirling a stray tendril. A shy awkwardness assailed her, and she straightened, saying with the slightest tremor, "There you are, my lord...all done."

Nicolas groaned inwardly, swallowing his disappointment with an effort. Having Claire so near, and being unable to touch her, to make his desire for her known, was more hell than heaven. Gad, why had he chosen a maid whose good opinion mattered to him? And why should her good opinion matter?

He stood, slanting a cursory glance at his reflection in the mirror. He peered closer. "Very nice work, Claire," he admired. "'Tis scarcely noticeable."

Claire beamed shyly, obviously pleased at his compliment. She looked so sweet, so irresistible. Good opinions be damned, thought Nicolas, and swept her into his arms for a quick, tight embrace. He touched a light kiss to the silky skin of her neck and set her away. "Thank you."

"Not at all," she murmured, her eyes alight with a soft glow. She fussed a moment with her gown and smoothed her palms down her skirt. "Are we ready to go, then?"

"Yes, I rather think we are." Nicolas smiled, pulled on his gloves and offered his arm. Though obviously flustered, Claire hadn't disliked his embrace, which encouraged him. Mmm, and holding her against him engendered a very nice sensation.

Fifteen minutes later, they were on the road to Dover in a black coach with the Kenton coat of arms emblazoned on the door. Their designated coachman sat on the box, while John rode alongside with pistols tucked beneath his coat. Nicolas glanced at a side pocket of the coach where his own weapon waited primed and ready.

He rather thought it fruitless to hope he might catch a glimpse of the two ruffians whilst in Dover. However, if he did see them, he didn't know how he'd engage in exchanging shots with Claire in tow. He sighed. He'd sent a letter to Renshaw at first light by private messenger, knowing that man would not be pleased to learn the traitors had slipped through his fingers. It could take an army of men to have such luck again.

"I've instructed the coachman to drive about the town, to show you the sights, Claire, and John has volunteered to ride alongside," Nicolas said upon reaching the outskirts. "Afterwards, I thought we might take lunch—" at a reputable inn this time, he thought "—and then perhaps you'd like to visit the shops?"

Claire nodded. "I'd like that, thank you. I've heard much about the wharf district . . . all the great ships coming and going—I'm eager to see them."

Nicolas smiled. *Good.* Dover was one of England's busiest ports, and if he had any chance of seeing his men, 'twould be there. He leaned closer to the window, pointing out such attractions as might amuse Claire, his gaze keen and hawklike upon the participants in the scene.

Claire took enthusiastic delight in the view, exclaiming in particular over a large merchantman with colourful, brawny sailors working on deck. Nicolas smiled at her interest and gave a short discourse on where the ship likely came from and what goods it might carry. However, a stirring of disappointment assailed him at the sure realisation that he wouldn't find his men.

By the time they stopped for lunch, Nicolas was thoroughly bored with his quest and even rather vexed. Damned frustrating, knowing that those who sought his life had escaped so prettily from his hands. But he could do nought about it now, save fuss. Choosing to dismiss the issue, he instead set out to charm his lovely wife.

Claire settled into the private parlour Nicolas bespoke for lunch, untying the ribbons of her bonnet and placing it on a nearby settee. She found herself in charity with Nicolas for suggesting this outing. Although he seemed in something of a brown study, he was, nevertheless, an informative guide. She now knew more of Dover than she'd ever thought possible. However, his preoccupation concerned her, and she wondered if it had anything to do with his injuries from last evening.

"Thank you, my lord," she said after the covers of their meal were lifted. "I'm enjoying myself immensely. I hope it hasn't been too tedious for you, escorting me about the town?"

Nicolas shook his head. "Not at all, my lady. Only an idiot would not enjoy your company." His lips tilted upwards. "And I'm not an idiot."

Claire's heart palpated a bit faster and her breath caught in her throat. Was he flirting with her? The knowledge was heady. Still, she wouldn't be swayed from her course. Gently she pried, "But you seem a bit... burdened?"

He covered her hand with his. "Claire, I confess I haven't been the most congenial company." He raised her hand, kissing her fingertips. "I apologise, and from this moment forth, will exert myself to be a charming companion."

Claire smiled, but wasn't at all taken in by his pretty speech. Nicolas did have something on his mind, something he was loath to share with her. She rather thought wild horses wouldn't drag his secret from him. She was curious beyond measure, but decided a dutiful wife would probably leave her husband to his own counsel.

He cradled her hand in his warm, larger one, and though the sensation was pleasant, and now not in the least alarming, she still needed that member to finish her meal. She withdrew it gently and lifted her fork. "You've been a most informative companion today, Nicolas. Still, I can't help but think something is troubling you. I collect that you don't care to share it with me, but I should like you to know I can be trusted."

"Thank you, Claire. It's heartening to know I haven't married a rattle." Nicolas held her gaze for several long moments. Yes, he was thankful he hadn't married a rattle, but oh, how much easier a rattle might have been to deal with! His dream of a wife who kept to her own business was rapidly crumbling. If Claire continued with her questioning, he'd soon resort to lies, and more lies; that, or else be abrupt with her—hardly a good foundation for a blissful union either way.

Realising she waited for something more from him, Nicolas cleared his throat and sighed. "I wouldn't dream of spoiling your outing with my worries. Now tell me, is the meal to your liking?"

Claire stared hard at him. Dropping her gaze, she nodded her satisfaction. Nicolas shrank inwardly at the certain knowledge that he risked any tender emotions she might be learning in his regard.

Later, Claire browsed through the goods displayed in the general mercantile, always entertained at viewing the new items on the market. She seldom purchased anything, and rarely found something she simply could not be without. Bolts of cloth on a table near the rear of the store caught her attention. Nicolas viewed an assortment of hats, seemingly content to allow her to mosey at will, so she headed towards the material.

A fine silk, shot with a rainbow of colours caught her attention. She admired the material, running it between her fingers, but soon dismissed it as unsuitable for anything she might need. However, she found a durable nankeen selling at a remarkably low price. Reasoning that surely several of Nicolas's tenants could use such cloth for their childrens' winter comfort, she scooped up the bolt, intent on purchasing the lot. Fanny had once remarked at the number of children Nicolas's tenants had.

"Oh, m'lady, m'lady!" the store owner stammered, fluttering over. "Do let me carry that for you! How much did you want?"

"I want it all," Claire replied. Nicolas glanced up from his perusal of the hats. "You don't mind, do you, Nicolas?" she asked. "The material is quite inexpensive, and I rather thought your tenants could use it...."

He regarded her with a strange look in his eyes. "Of course I don't mind, but Claire, I distinctly saw you admiring that . . . that other pretty material over there." He gestured to the silk. "Don't you want it?"

"Oh, 'tis very beautiful," Claire responded, "but I'm sure I haven't the slightest use for it. Why, your mama commissioned enough gowns for my trousseau to keep me outfitted forever!"

Again he studied her, then lifted one shoulder in a shrug. "I think that colour would look startling on you." He turned to the shopkeeper. "We'll take it, too."

The shopkeeper bowed in gratification, and moved to do his bidding. Claire stared at Nicolas, amazed. His kindness was disconcerting. The Nicolas she'd thought she'd married—Lord Iceberg Incarnate—was becoming the warm Nicolas of Fanny's description. Could his mother be right about him?

Claire made sure she was more than a trifle spoiled by her new husband. Heavens! Hadn't he received the notes from the modiste in London? A life of frugality hadn't prepared her for this free-handed spending. Some portion of her wanted to say she surely didn't need the material, but another voice reasoned it would be vulgar to argue. After all, it was Nicolas's money, and he could spend it as he wished. She satisfied herself by giving him a sweet smile and a simple "Thank you."

THE FOLLOWING DAYS passed as quickly as a hawk diving for prey. Nicolas took her to visit his tenants, showed her the farms, and spoke of his hopes for the future development of his lands. Claire listened avidly, more to the deep timbre of love for his home she heard in his voice, than to the actual details of his plans.

Nicolas, the perfect gentleman, was—yes—even charming as Fanny had said. He hadn't once approached her on the subject of his heir, and though she was thankful for that consideration, still, it confused her. Had she offended him in some way? Or was he simply not tempted to come to her bed? She gave thought to how she might feel if he did come to her, and decided she'd best appreciate what freedom she had. True, he was more familiar to her, and not so frightening, but the idea of being *that* intimate with him was still a daunting prospect.

However, she did her best to be a good wife in other ways. She discovered Nicolas's favourite meals and requested their preparation. She toured the house with Mrs. Trumble, inspecting those areas Nicolas had neglected to show her, such things as the linen closets and the scullery. Overused linen was borne away and utilised in less dignified ways, for cleaning rags and the like. Fresh lavender added to the closets scented the remainder.

All in all, Claire found herself remarkably content. Only one thing plagued her. Several times she'd gone outdoors to tend to the herb garden or smell the roses. On every occasion, John the groom had dogged her steps. Oh, he'd attempted to make himself inconspicuous, and only came forth when she remarked his presence with a "Good day to you, John."

Still, she thought it rather queer that he'd spy on her, and the knowledge that he carried a pistol made her quite uneasy. She thought to quiz Nicolas about this odd behaviour, but couldn't like creating a problem at this early stage of her new role as countess.

Today she and Nicolas were off to visit Leo, a tenant reported as not working for some days. Sundance and Nicolas's huge bay, Apollo, were saddled and waiting. Nicolas assisted Claire into the saddle, and vaulted atop his horse. Rather than showing anger at his tenant's slothfulness, he seemed concerned.

"It's not like Leo to shirk his responsibilities," Nicolas said, urging Apollo from the yard.

Claire had seen enough to know Nicolas was indeed a worthy landowner. His farms were in excellent condition, and his tenants seemed to want for little. Nicolas, she'd noticed, kept his eyes open for any sign of distress, offering help before they asked.

"I'm not sure I've met Leo and his family," she ventured, stroking Sundance's velvet neck.

"No. I rather thought all was in order with them on my last visit, which wasn't long ago. Shall we canter? I admit to being rather concerned."

Claire nodded, lifting the reins and giving Sundance leave to break into the faster gait. The mare was a dream. Claire admired her smooth, even stride. Now, though, her attention focused on Nicolas. She wondered how many hundreds of tenants might desire him for their landlord. He was good to them, and more than that, he was kind. She'd seen in but a few days how these qualities were well respected by his people.

Sparing a glance across at him, she noted the dark locks tumbling in windswept abandon, the grey eyes narrowed against the breeze. He rode athletically, his hands light on the reins, his strong thighs hugging his mount. He sent her an enquiring grin, and her gaze sidled away.

A sudden stab of sadness struck her at the thought that he hadn't found a wife who could love him. Surely he deserved such a woman. A tiny voice in her head challenged, *You're his wife. Why can't you love him?* She pushed the question aside, for after all, her heart was already given to Robert.

A few minutes later, they pulled up in front of a neat farmhouse, which exuded an appealing orderliness, though the atmosphere definitely was hushed. No sooner did Nicolas lift her from the saddle than the door opened. A pleasingly plump woman came out of the house, wringing her hands on the apron tied about her waist. Five little children emerged behind her.

"Oh, yer lordship!" she exclaimed, obviously agitated. "Leo would've been to work, honestly he would've. He's a good man, that he is, and wouldn't no more'n cheat you than your blessed mama! I'm at sixes and sevens, and don't know what to do! He said as how he'd be goin' back to work but I misdoubt it, what with the fever comin' on and all."

"Nance," said Nicolas, holding up a hand to halt her outpouring. "I know Leo would never cheat me, so do put yourself at rest." He drew Claire forward, saying, "I should like you to meet my countess."

Nance gave a flustered bob. "I'm that pleased to meet your ladyship. I hope you don't take me for an addle-pate, as I did notice you immediately, so pretty you are. 'Tis just that I'm that worried for my poor Leo."

"That's understandable," Claire said graciously. "Your concern for your husband is laudable. Pray tell what ails him?"

Nicolas started for the open door, ruffling the short red crops of the several children he was forced to dodge on his way.

Claire followed, as Nance's tale of woe resumed. "I say he broke his leg when he took that fall two days ago, but he won't have nothin' of it. But he can't walk and now he has the fever, and he swore he'd be better in a few days, but I never did think so. He says he can't have broke his leg 'cause he needs to work to feed the babes, and I'm tellin' him that's the greatest nonsense because if he broke his leg, he broke his leg and we'll survive somehow, though I don't see how that may be..."

Nicolas ducked inside the door with Claire and Nance close behind. A man lay on a cot before the hearth, his eyes shut against his obvious pain. Nicolas squatted beside him, saying, "Leo, my good fellow, I'll have a look at that leg, if you please."

"I've told her it ain't broke, yer lordship," Leo ground out through clenched teeth. "I'll be right as rain in a day or so and be back to the fields—you'll see."

"That's as may be, Leo, but I still wish to see the leg." Nicolas drew back the coverlet in spite of the man's protests, revealing the bruised and swollen ankle. He swore softly under his breath. "Leo, why wasn't I informed of this immediately?"

The man looked a bit abashed, peering past Nicolas to Claire. "I didn't want to bother yer lordship, what with you being newly wedded and all."

"That's no excuse, Leo. And do meet my countess, Lady Kenton." He drew Claire forward, and she acknowledged the introduction. "I trust," Nicolas continued, "that in the future I'll be informed of all injuries post-haste—and that injunction includes the entirety of your family. Is that clear?"

"Yes, m'lord."

"Good. I shall send for the doctor, and you're to obey his instructions explicitly. And do rest assured that you and your family will be taken care of." His features softened and he laid a hand on the man's shoulder. "Understand?"

Leo managed a weak smile. "Yes, yer lordship. And thank you."

"Not at all." Nicolas turned to Nance, putting his arm round her shoulder and guiding her to the table. "I know of a hard-working youth who can help with the chores. Leo will be abed for some time, that much is clear. If you have any needs, you'll be sure to bring them to me, won't you?"

"Oh, yes, m'lord. And thank you ever so much." Nance wiped a tear from her eye and sighed gustily, as if she'd been relieved of a great burden.

"Now, Lady Kenton has purchased some nankeen, which we'll send over later, along with a basket of goods. Do you lack for anything else?" Nicolas enquired kindly.

"No, m'lord, we're that grateful."

Nicolas nodded. "Then expect the doctor soon. We'll come by again to see how you fare."

Claire and Nicolas left the house amid a chorus of "thank yous" and "bless yous". They waved to the children straggling out behind them, and turned their mounts towards home.

"I can scarce credit he's lain there for two days without anything for pain!" Nicolas said in tones of disbelief and anger, shaking his head. "That ankle needs setting, and he needs a good dose of laudanum."

"He also needs a posset to bring down that swelling," Claire replied, already preparing a healing potion of sorts in her head.

"Tell me, do you suppose you might get Cook to prepare a package of goods whilst I see the doctor summoned? Poor souls, it can't be easy for them, wondering how they'll fare through the next weeks. I'll try to make it as easy as possible for them."

"It shouldn't take me long," she said, "but we'd best step up the pace. I can't imagine Leo is all too comfortable."

Nicolas inclined his head, and urged Apollo into a gallop. Claire followed suit, marvelling at his generosity towards the couple. Yes, Nicolas was kind, thoughtful and efficient—certainly a man worthy of her respect, even if she couldn't give him her heart.

CHAPTER NINE

THREE DAYS LATER, Claire made for the stables, holding the skirt of her forest green riding habit in one hand, and clutching a parcel of herbs she intended to take to Nance in the other. Nicolas awaited her, handsome in buckskin breeches and a Spanish blue coat. He smiled at her approach, extending a hand for her parcel before assisting her to mount.

Claire returned his smile, finding warm pleasure in that Nicolas truly seemed to enjoy her presence. She almost felt wanted, and not for anything but herself. It was a novel sensation, and one she was loath to study in too much detail. Nicolas swung into his saddle with a lean, athletic grace. Claire admired his form and balance as much on this occasion as she had on several others.

"I find myself desiring a good gallop," he said, lifting a challenging brow. "Are you game?"

Claire smiled, giving one short, firm nod. She leant over Sundance with a sharp click of her tongue. Sundance gathered herself and shot forward, leaving Apollo to follow in her wake. Claire laughed with delight, knowing an equal mixture of unabandoned freedom and joy at having bested Nicolas.

Nicolas's rumble of laughter came from behind. Seconds later Apollo shot ahead of the smaller Sundance. "A race!" he shouted. "To yonder tree. First one there wins a prize!"

"No fair!" Claire cried, already knowing who the loser would be. She leaned into Sundance and whispered a fierce, "Go, girl! Beat that old Apollo!"

Sundance responded with what she had, which, unfortunately, didn't match Apollo's mettle. He cleared the tree lengths ahead. Claire drew up beside Nicolas, bubbling with laughter. "Very well, my lord, you win. What shall your prize be?"

"You get to carry this packet of herbs." He lifted the forgotten parcel, grinning. Nudging Apollo closer, he turned in the saddle and leant towards her, brandishing the package.

Simultaneously, a loud crack split the morning air and reverberated through the quiet countryside.

Nicolas gasped and rocked back, the herbs falling from his hand. Before Claire realised she'd heard a pistol shot, he'd grabbed at Sundance's reins and tugged on Apollo's, turning them about. "Home, Claire, as fast as you can!"

He whacked Sundance neatly on the rump, and urged Apollo after her. Another report sounded, mingling with the pounding of hooves, and the thudding of Claire's heart. Merciful God, whatever was happening? And Nicolas, why wasn't he beside her, instead of riding behind? He was protecting her back! But what about himself?

The stableyard had never been so inviting. She and Nicolas galloped in, bringing their sweating mounts to a thundering halt.

"John!" Nicolas shouted. "John!"

Claire didn't wait to be helped down. She slid off Sundance's back and ran to Nicolas, who gingerly removed himself from Apollo's. "Oh, Nicolas, your shoulder! You *were* shot! It all happened so fast I couldn't be sure!"

John ran out of the stables. Nicolas sent him a piercing stare. "Poachers, I make no doubt. Damned bad shots, too. Gather some men and see what you can find—be sure to determine if any of the local lads were out today. We were at the lone fir. Report back immediately you learn anything."

John nodded and ran back into the stable, shouting for his undergrooms. Nicolas turned to Claire, and enfolded her in a one-armed embrace. Claire rested her head on his shoulder, finding comfort in the beat of his heart and his warm nearness.

Nicolas smoothed his hand down her back, pulling her close, as if gaining the same measure of reassurance from her proximity. After some moments, he eased her gently away. "I'm sorry, Claire. Are you all right?"

Claire drew a deep breath and slowly exhaled. Shaken and trembling, she was otherwise none the worse for the experience. She nodded. "But we need to get you inside and determine the extent of that wound. It's not bleeding overmuch, but I daresay it must pain."

"Yes, it does burn a trifle, though I doubt it's more than a flesh wound. Come, then." He placed a hand at her back, and guided her through the door. Clark hurried up, asking what was amiss. Nicolas briefly explained their mishap, and commissioned him to find a footman to retrieve and deliver the herbs to Leo.

Claire added an order for water and necessary bandaging supplies, and turned Nicolas towards the stairs and his chambers. Once inside, she helped him remove his coat. She knew the action gave him some pain, but he uttered not a sound.

The blood pooled thicker on his white shirt, creating a large and gruesome stain about his shoulder. Claire's stomach lurched at the sight. She lifted her eyes to his face, flicking her tongue over suddenly dry lips. Summoning her strongest voice, she said, "Nicolas, do you realise—"

"That if I hadn't turned to you in that precise second, I'd be dead? Yes, Claire, I do." His fingers caressed the soft skin under her chin. "Thank God for your herbs."

His grey gaze held her spellbound for what seemed endless moments. Claire lost herself in the timeless magic of the moment. A sharp rapping at the door shattered the sweet rapport.

She dragged her gaze from his, and Nicolas uttered an impatient exclamation. "Come!"

A turning of the knob met his brusque summons. The door opened, revealing a timid Maggie bearing a tray of water and bandaging materials. She took one look at Nicolas's countenance and set the tray on a small table. Bobbing a hasty curtsy, she fled.

Nicolas looked at Claire, giving a half shrug with his good shoulder. "I daresay we should tend this arm."

He fumbled with the buttons of his shirt. Claire came out of her spell and moved to help him, brushing his fingers aside and using both her hands to make quick work of the buttons. Her fingers inadvertently trailed against the warm skin of his chest and taut midriff. She kept her head lowered for fear her awareness of him might show on her face.

Nicolas extricated his good arm from the sleeve, and Claire carefully pulled the shirt away from his wound and off the other. The wound was ugly, true, but it wasn't that which made her catch her breath. She'd never seen a man's bare chest, and the sight of Nicolas, naked to his lean, slender waist aroused a response in her she hadn't expected.

Mercy! He resembled a splendid work of art. Muscled arms and wide shoulders gave way to a broad expanse of chest, beautifully formed. A sprinkling of hairs created a star in the centre, tapering all the way down his torso to disappear beneath the waistline of his breeches.

A trembling seized her, more powerful than any she'd experienced on their wild ride home. *Gather yourself, Claire Elizabeth!* She tore her gaze from the awesome sight and turned quickly towards the bandage tray, clutching the folds of her habit to steady her shaking hands.

A potent urge to run her fingers over his warm flesh gripped her like the ague. Heavens, what was happening to her? She loved Robert, didn't she? Then why, oh why, did this man have the power to rob her of all reason? It was sheer madness, she admonished herself, sheer, lustful madness.

She made a pretence of arranging the supplies, giving herself several more seconds to find composure. Moving the small table near a chair, she bade Nicolas sit. She kept her eyes averted from his, and groped for words to break the awkwardness.

"The poachers, Nicolas. Surely they wouldn't have mistaken you for an animal? Why, that is absurd! There were two shots! I doubt I would be far off to say it was done on purpose."

Nicolas coughed, then groaned as the spasm rocked his shoulder. After several long moments, he ventured, "I daresay that could be possible, Claire, but there are likely any number of explanations. A shot gone awry, perhaps, or a lad just learning the use of a fire-arm. Perhaps they didn't see us. Nevertheless, I think it prudent to limit our wanderings to the gardens, at least until the mystery is solved. You will stay close, won't you?"

"Oh, yes." Claire readily agreed, having no desire to leave the confines of the gardens. Bad shots, boys, or what-have-you left her shaken enough to want nothing more than the safe security of her home. 'Twas probably as Nicolas said, some lad testing his mettle with a weapon, but still, she didn't wish to take chances.

As gently as she might, she washed the blood from his shoulder and fixed her attention upon the wound itself. Nicolas bore her ministrations with stoicism. Once the wound was cleaned to her satisfaction, she lifted the portion of brandy included on the tray.

"This is going to sting," she warned, dribbling the brandy thoroughly over his wound. Nicolas hissed through his teeth, bearing up against the pain. Claire grimaced. "I'm sorry. Are you all right? I'm almost finished," she said at his tight nod. "I only need to bandage it."

She made quick work with the strips of linen, wrapping them around Nicolas's shoulder so they'd remain secure even whilst he slept. With a final pat to her handiwork, she stepped back, at last looking him in the face. "Any better?"

"That cursed brandy is foul stuff," was Nicolas's reply. "But yes, and thank you for your ministrations."

His gaze caressed her face, the light in his eyes warm and beckoning. Claire turned hastily to his wardrobe. "I'll find you a shirt."

Nicolas watched her walk away, inhaling the last of her sweet perfume before it evaporated in the air. *Damn!* How much longer was he to live with her so close and yet be denied the pleasure of touching her? Allowing her to nurse him, her soft, cool hands brushing his burning flesh, her perfume teasing his nose, without so much as smoothing the tendrils back from her face, required more control than he'd known he possessed.

He wanted to rush his fences, get closer and take her lips in the most searing kiss he'd ever given a woman. The urge proved too strong. He rose from his chair and followed her with a deceptive lack of haste. She turned, gasped at his proximity and thrust his shirt forward. Nicolas took it from her nerveless grasp, slung it over his shoulder and gathered her into his embrace.

Startled, she stiffened. An advantageous action, for her gaze flew to him, thus tilting her head for the onslaught of his lips. He buried his hand in her hair, slanted his mouth across hers and kissed her—long and hungrily. He didn't mind her lack of response. This time he was prepared.

He reached for her hand, capturing it, bringing it to his chest and trailing it down in a sensual exploration. His tongue flicked between her lips which were parted in shock, teasing the tip of hers before delving further. Her mouth softened against his, her body melted to him, and she grew limp in his arms.

Suddenly he returned to reality, feeling as if he'd been doused with a bucket of icy water. *By all that's holy,* he thought, *she's swooned!* He tore his mouth from hers, his eyes flying open.

You're a blithering idiot, Nicolas Shea! he cursed himself. So much for wooing her gently! And things *had* been going fairly well! He held his wife in his arms, preventing her from sliding to the floor at his feet. Rejection stabbed at him, hotter and sharper than he'd ever experienced. She didn't want him, or his kisses.

Her lashes rested against her flushed cheeks. Slowly they lifted, and she stared at him as if dazed. Seeming to recall herself, she immediately straightened up, her fingers rising to touch her swollen lips.

"Why did you do that?" she asked in a weak voice.

Nicolas closed his eyes for one painful second. Had she indeed swooned, or had she responded? Had he been so shocked that he'd merely *thought* she'd swooned? He didn't dare to ask. "I lost my head," he muttered, his tones husky and apologetic. "I'm sorry."

Claire wasn't. She'd never experienced a more soul-shattering interlude. Her legs were weak, and she gave thanks for his supporting arms. Her entire body had desired to meld into his. The room, and indeed, the world had spun away when his tongue entered her mouth. Her every sense had become blind and deaf to all but him— his kisses, the delightful feel of warm skin and muscle beneath her fingertips, the guidance and protection of his hand over hers.

She hadn't known a kiss could stir such fires as kindled inside her. Her surrender to his drugging embrace had been complete. And she hadn't wanted to know why he'd kissed her, but why he'd ceased to do so. She opened her mouth to ask him to continue, and realised she couldn't, did not dare. Not only that, but what maggot had got into her head? Did she actually want to kiss him *again*?

Really, Claire Elizabeth, she admonished herself, *you are a peagoose. This is Nicolas . . . your husband . . . your unwanted husband.* Whatever was she thinking? But the sight of him, his features softened in the aftermath of their kiss, was the most appealing picture she'd ever seen. She straightened with a jerk, sternly quelling her wayward thoughts.

"Do . . . do you need help with your shirt?"

"Yes, I suppose so," he murmured, his quiet, well-modulated tones once more in evidence.

She took the garment, gently easing his wounded arm through the sleeve. His face was now a shuttered mask. She considered him silently, wishing he would catch her gaze, and wishing he would not. Her fingers touched his warm torso, and she trembled. Merciful heavens! How could one kiss so shatter a lady's composure? Even worse, she wanted to kiss him again, and that she couldn't deny. She hooked the final button and backed towards the door connecting her chamber with his.

"Excuse me," she murmured, and turned and fled, not caring if she made a cake of herself. He'd put her nerves all about with that unexpected, and devastating kiss.

WEEDING THE HERB GARDEN, Claire gave vent to roiling emotions. 'Twas a mindless task, leaving her thoughts free to flow in directions she would as lief not consider, but deemed necessary. What was wrong with her? Did she so lack pride that she would instantly melt in Nicolas's arms? He'd bought her, so whyever would she desire his kisses... indeed, crave them? Was she so fickle? She loved Robert, didn't she? Then how could she surrender to Nicolas's embrace? And why did it feel so right, so warm... so good? It was too vexing. Her emotions were too disorderly, too contrary. Oh, what she would give for the peaceful heart she'd had before their jaunt to London. Things had seemed so simple then.

She plucked a shoot, realised it wasn't a weed and sighed. What was it about Nicolas that made chaos of her thoughts? True, he was handsome and virile, and yes, kind and sensitive. And he'd protected her back today on their wild flight home. He'd also had a care for her reputation that night at Hyde Park—as Robert hadn't.

She'd escaped unscathed from both situations, thanks to Nicolas. He might have died today. Her heart lurched unpleasantly at the thought. Had John found the poachers? Were they only lads, as Nicolas suggested? Her hand stopped as it reached for another weed. The beach, the fight, the trip to Dover... his unwillingness to part with any information crowded her mind... were they all tied together? Did someone want her husband dead?

NICOLAS, restless and bored, and more than a trifle vexed at his confinement, strolled outdoors, making for the herb garden where he knew Claire worked. Some paces away, he stopped and regarded his wife. She lifted a finger to scratch her nose, leaving a smear of dirt on her flawless white skin. He smiled. She looked so... at home...so comfortable, like his grandmother when she'd tended her beloved garden. She would have approved of Claire.

Claire... so different from what he'd first imagined. She wasn't at all a City Belle, like Penelope. Where Penelope had revelled in the attention she received, Claire had stood back, graciously, but modestly, accepting any courtesies she attracted. Claire wasn't *brassy*.

Penelope would have hated Kenwood Park. Even the thought of life with her—staying overlong in London, the routs, the balls, the musicales which gave Penelope endless pleasure—made him shudder. Claire, on the other hand, seemed more than content to be in the country.

Never would Penelope have considered soiling her hands with a herb garden. Nor would she have chosen nankeen over silk, thinking first of others before herself. Whatever had he seen in her? Her beauty... her charm, be it ever so superficial.

Claire had no need for such deceptions. She was honestly refreshing, her company truly pleasurable. Undemanding, plainspoken, generous, caring. He rather thought his mama was right: he doubted he could have done any better for himself.

And Claire was proving to be a good wife: he'd enjoyed his favourite meals; his bedclothes were unmistakably fresher. The servants liked her, and already his tenants accorded her a genuine respect. She was indeed remarkable, and he was proud to have her as his wife. He'd chosen with good sense.

Only one thing more might he have wished from her: a willingness to accept the intimate aspects of their marriage. Kissing her today had only intensified his longing to know all of her. He was as hot-blooded as any man, and living in such proximity to a beautiful woman nearly sapped his control.

And damn, he needed that heir. The throbbing shoulder wound gave blatant testimony that his life stood in ever-increasing danger. He almost felt vulnerable standing in his own yard, even knowing his men patrolled the area.

He'd received a missive from Renshaw this morning, enquiring whether he'd had any news of Robert. They needed that list, with all haste; the traitors to the Crown must be found. Not only was the enemy closing in on Nicolas, but matters were becoming unstable in the War Office. Information wasn't getting through.

A silent sigh escaped Nicolas's lips. Robert still hadn't returned. Was he alive? What would England do if he failed to locate Andrew? And how long might he, Nicolas, remain safe? The threat to his life loomed like an impending storm, and he had yet to accomplish his primary goal for taking a wife.

He studied Claire contemplatively. Her old grey frock only emphasised her beauty. He couldn't deny he wanted her as badly as he wanted an heir. A part of him urged that he have his way with her, regardless of her wishes. But another, stronger voice demanded he respect her feelings. How could he force his will upon her when she'd taken such pains to be a perfect countess in all other ways?

He couldn't. Her feelings in the matter must be considered. But how on earth was he to beget an heir? Had he sabotaged all his efforts of the past weeks by kissing her today? Or had she responded? And if she had, then why did she rush from him as if the demons of hell were at her heels? What could he do? What else could he possibly try to bring her about, to wrest her heart from Robert West?

He'd tried to woo her. He'd given his time, his money. All he had was hers. He'd have to double his efforts, but how? He searched his mind, and hit on the one thing he'd forgotten: the family jewels. How remiss of him! Claire was bound to find delight in the glittering mass of gems, perhaps even enough to melt through her icy reserve. It was worth a try—anything was. Nicolas retraced his steps, making his way towards the safe where his last hope of thawing Claire awaited him.

CLAIRE DRESSED with care for dinner. Emma arranged her hair in a becoming chignon, coaxing stray tendrils to curl about her face. A red satin gown swirled to her ankles, and she could only wish the décolletage were as modest. Cut daringly low, the bodice showed more of her bosom than she deemed seemly.

Emma didn't set her fears to rest. Staring rapturously with her hands clasped to her chest, she declared his

lordship would be that pleased. Claire ardently wished
for a shawl, but knew it wouldn't serve. Not only would
one spoil the effect of the gown, but Emma would be sure
to fuss.

Claire joined Nicolas in the drawing-room, and immediately wished she had insisted on the shawl. His gaze
slid in slow exploration from the ivory comb in her hair
to the tips of her red satin slippers. She straightened her
shoulders, refusing to blush at the admiration she
glimpsed in his eyes. He stepped forward, taking her
hand and raising it to his lips.

"Red becomes you exceedingly, my lady," he murmured. "Come, I fear I've neglected a most important
husbandly duty." His smile caressed her, and he raised
one thumb, drawing it from her jawline down her neck.
Tiny tremors of delight rippled through her, and she
caught her breath.

He turned, moving across the room to a large enam-
elled case. "I beg your forgiveness, but I've been terribly remiss. The family jewels are yours to command.
Though they're kept in a vault in the study, you need only
ask for them."

Flicking back the latch on the case, he opened it to
display a pirate's treasure. Jewels of all shapes and colours sparkled up at Claire, and she gasped with awe.

"Oh, Nicolas, they're lovely," she breathed, lifting
several pieces for closer inspection. A sapphire brooch,
an emerald ring and a diamond earring winked at her in
the candlelight.

Nicolas sorted through the case, bringing forth two
glorious necklaces. "Should you like the diamonds or the
rubies for tonight?" he asked. "I daresay they each have
matching earrings . . . somewhere in here."

Claire bit her lip in indecision. "Oh, they're both so beautiful, I'm sure I can't choose! Perhaps the diamonds, as I'm already wearing so much red?"

"The diamonds will be stunning," Nicolas assured her. "Ah, and here are the earrings. Come, I'll help you put them on." He laid aside the case and, taking her hand, led her to the large mirror set between two equally large paintings.

Claire affixed the earrings and reached for the necklace, but saw her husband had other plans. He unfastened the clasp and placed the dazzling piece around her neck. She stood utterly still. The cool gems settled with unaccustomed weight on her neck, but the warmth of his fingers as he worked the clasp held her attention.

He smoothed the sparkling jewels about her collarbone, his fingers splaying across her flesh. Her lashes drifting down, she marvelled at the sensations claiming her. Facing the mirror as they were, she saw his head lower. His lips touched her neck in a gentle kiss. Her breath caught, and she forced herself to expel it. He looked up, and their eyes met.

"Stunning," he murmured, his fingers trailing hot brands of fire down her neck to the curve of her breast. She regarded him silently, knowing an impulse to lean back against him and an intense desire to have his fingers caress lower still.

"Dinner is served, my lord, my lady," Clark intoned behind them.

A scowl of impatience flashed across Nicolas's face. With a tiny sigh of resignation, he stepped away and offered his arm. Claire, wondering at her own sense of disappointment, turned and rested her hand lightly on his sleeve. They went into the dining room without speaking.

"Clark," Nicolas said the moment they entered, "I'd have you move my wife's setting to the place beside me. You can hardly expect me to behold her beauty down miles of table, especially with that hideous vase to obscure my vison."

Clark mastered a smile, and made a stately bow. "As you wish, m'lord. I shall be but a moment."

Nicolas led Claire to his end of the table, pulling a chair for her at his right. Leaning close to her ear, and trailing a finger down her neck, he whispered, "You're far more luscious to look upon than any food they could serve."

His words tickled Claire's ear, and a quiver of excitement tingled through her. She sent him a shy glance, and looked away, knowing she blushed. Was this the man who had so coldly proposed to her in the tiny garden of her London house—the man who desired not even a modicum of affection from his spouse? What was he about?

The questions roiled round her brain, confusing her as much as his effect on her senses. His attentions pleased her. Yes, pleased, and she needn't deny it. She lifted her soup spoon, not knowing what she might say.

Nicolas took the task from her, confusing her even more by the nonchalance of his address. "They found no sign of the poachers, so I think it best to keep close to home for a time. I don't mind, as I rather desired having you to myself for a spell."

Claire peered at him from beneath her lashes. He wanted her to himself? What game was he playing at? The answer flashed upon her, like lightning illuminating a dark night. Of course! He wished to coax her into his bed with sweetness and pretty words, instead of by force.

While one part of her gave him credit for not being a brute, another argued that his motives were hardly pure. Well, if he thought for one moment to cozen her, he was decidedly mistaken. His pretty affections were all for show, initiated to bring her about to being a willing brood mare.

She dipped her soup spoon, feeling oddly deflated. She'd almost believed he'd come to like her. And perhaps he did, a little. But his actions bespoke his quest of an heir . . . and they'd become all the more pronounced after the shooting mishap.

The remainder of dinner passed well. Nicolas made light and easy conversation. In spite of herself, Claire enjoyed his company, laughing at his many witticisms. But her head reminded her that his pleasantries were for a purpose: his precious heir. Some errant gallantry in him demanded he not make love to a martyr.

The last course was removed, and she retired to the drawing-room, leaving her husband to his port. Selecting a chair, she lifted the book she'd been reading, but got only as far as opening it. Her gaze travelled about the room, resting on nothing. Prey to an equally restless mind, she didn't realise she'd worried the pages of the book until a corner of paper tore off in her fingers. She stared at the frayed piece, and squeezed her eyes shut.

She actually found her husband charming. More than that, she looked to be in his company, and desired his touch. It was too confusing. Her head told her he merely wanted an heir, but her heart, it seemed, wouldn't listen. She waited, and indeed, wished, for every touch Nicolas might give her. She berated herself for a peagoose, but yet . . . he was so near, so warm, so wonderful. . . .

Nicolas strolled into the room. She dropped the frayed corner between the pages of the book and shut it. A tremulous, uncertain smile hovered on her lips.

"Would you care for a walk in the garden, Claire?"

She set the book aside, and stood up in a rush. Anything was preferable to sitting here idle. "I should like that, Nicolas."

He reached for her hand. She gave it without flinching. A satisfied, even happy, smile tugged at his mouth. He led her through the garden doors, down the terrace steps and into the fragrant night.

Claire strolled beside him, content to be with him, to have her hand held in his gentle, yet firm, clasp. At the rose bushes, Nicolas halted. He plucked a bloom, stripped it of thorns and turned to her.

"A flower for your hair, my dear?" he asked, a nonsensical grin playing on his lips.

She smiled and nodded. He tucked the red rose in her hair, securing it with the ivory comb. The moonlight splayed across the garden, touching his handsome features and throwing shadows in the curves and hollows of his face. She admired the portrait he presented, watching his eyes grow darker. Snared in the moment, Claire awaited his next action.

He raised his hand, trailing a finger across her mouth. She nearly melted into his touch. She couldn't fight it. She wanted to, perhaps needed to. But she couldn't. She lifted her chin, knowing she wanted him to kiss her and wishing he would. She castigated herself for being every sort of a fool, for having no resolve, no proof against him. His face inched closer, and she thought her heart would burst into a thousand pinpricks of light. His mouth met hers, softly, gently. She swayed against him, her lips parted in silent invitation.

He gathered her to him, and she melded to his frame, delighting in every hard fibre of his physique. The kiss, at first tender and light, deepened. With a will beyond her own, Claire gave herself up to it, marvelling in the wonderment of his lips on hers, of the taste of his tongue as it flicked between her lips. She trembled everywhere, and wanted only for him to continue this onslaught of passion.

Nicolas could scarce believe her response. She was accepting his kisses, and returning them! His heart sang a hundred tunes. Never had a kiss tasted so sweet, never had his head reeled with such wanting for a woman's charms, and never had he known how very much he must constrain himself. He wanted to bed her in the garden, and to hell with propriety! Only the knowledge of her shy innocence held him in check. But it didn't stop him from caressing her back, her hips, from moving his hand hungrily to the inviting roundness of her breast.

He must remove to her chamber. He took regretful leave of her mouth, trailing his lips along her cheek, her brow, to the top of her head. His lashes flickered up for the briefest of instants. His gaze skimmed across the garden to the water beyond. A light bobbed, and disappeared. *West!* Curses! Double curses! And triple curses! Of all the blasted, ill-timed, rotten— Good God! West! He was alive!

"Claire," he said, seeking to control the urgency of his tone, "let us take ourselves inside, hmm?" At her bemused nod, he grasped her hand, stifling the desire to pull her along at a racer's pace.

Once inside her chamber, he lifted her, carrying her across the room and depositing her gently on the bed. Her hair tumbled about her face in wanton disarray, and he groaned. "God, you're beautiful."

He stepped back, knowing he must, now, because he wouldn't have the strength should he stay a second longer. Swift strides took him to the window where he whisked shut the curtains. What could he say? "We rush things, Claire."

The perplexed expression in her eyes arrested him.

"Sweet dreams," he whispered, and swivelled towards the connecting door without a backward glance, knowing that one more moment in her presence would have him consigning Robert West and his information to the devil.

CHAPTER TEN

CLAIRE STARED at the door, which had almost slammed shut behind Nicolas. Had she done something wrong? But what? Merciful heavens! She hadn't wanted him to stop! She wanted to call him back. She would have asked him to stay! Why did he go?

Nicolas! she raged. How could he ignite this conflagration inside her, then disappear? She got up and paced restlessly about the room, extinguishing the candles. His behaviour was absurd. Had he expected her to sleep, fully clothed, on top of the covers, and the room ablaze with light? He'd shut her curtains and rushed out. It was all too odd.

She stepped to the window, flicking back a corner of the curtain to survey the moonlit scene below. Catching a movement from the corner of her eye, she turned her head in time to see the figure of a man clearly etched in the moonlight. *Nicolas*—making for the Strait.

His form in the moonlight was easily discernible. His greatcoat whipped about his legs as he stood on the shore. The breeze ruffled his hair. Her stomach tightened at her awareness of his strength and virility.

She touched a finger to her lips, recalling their moments in the garden. What was happening to her? Were all kisses so magical, so entrancing that one knew nothing but a roar of emotion? Did all kisses incite one to cry for more? Her coldly dispassionate husband wasn't quite as icy as she'd imagined. He had hands and lips of fire, melting her resistance in a way she never could have dreamed of.

She'd thought when he took her, it would simply be that, a taking. She had never supposed she would want to give, to explore these delights with him. She'd never experienced such a longing and desire before, not even with Robert.

And what about Robert? And her good intentions? Yes, as his wife, she was honour bound to provide Nicolas an heir, but did she have to know this overwhelming physical response in the process? How could she possibly love one man, yet so desire another? Her body betrayed her heart, and the knowledge wasn't easy to own.

She frowned. Her mother had only told her a duty was a duty. It was not *unpleasant,* she'd said, but she'd never mentioned that your being could burst with a thousand stars, that your reason would desert you and that every nerve would tremble and tingle.

Claire sighed, peering across the expanse of garden and lawn. What was Nicolas doing? The water rippled, touched by silver moonlight, its surface smooth and unspoiled. Or was it? She pressed her face closer to the glass, her eyes narrowing. A boat? yes, and a man leaping from it to the sand. Nicolas clapped him on the back, and together they brought the craft in. Then they disappeared.

She stared for several long minutes, without catching so much as a glimpse of her husband and his comrade.

NICOLAS DIDN'T WAIT for Forsythe to help him dress. West had been so fatigued last night that Nicolas had declared his information could wait until morning. An alive and breathing West was good news in itself. Never had Nicolas dreamt he'd be so happy to see the man. But morning dawned, the sun steadily climbed the horizon, and if West wasn't up yet—he soon would be.

Nicolas tucked his shirt into his breeches and started for the door. Maggie bore a tray of chocolate down the hall. He paused. Maggie would wake Claire. Claire's hair would be tumbling about her face, her eyes would be sleepy...her mouth soft and tender. He'd never seen her when she'd first awoken. And he'd really made a muddle of it last night. By the time he'd seen West settled, her room was dark. It would have been too brutish to go to her then. But now...he couldn't resist. "Maggie, I will take my wife her chocolate this morning, thank you."

Maggie looked startled, but hastily handed over the tray. She bobbed two curtsies in quick succession. "Certainly, my lord. Thank you."

Nicolas tapped on Claire's chamber door. At her summons, he turned the knob and let himself into the room. Claire's gaze flew to him and a small gasp of astonishment left her lips.

"Nicolas." Her hand fluttered to her chest. A second later, she tugged the bedclothes up to her chin.

"Good morning, Claire," he murmured, smiling. Mercy, but she was the fairest lady on earth! Her hair all tumbled, her eyes wide and green with lingering traces of sleep. And her sweet, luscious lips...just as he had imagined. He cleared his throat, taming his wayward thoughts. "I confiscated your chocolate from Maggie. I thought I might enjoy bringing it to you this morning."

"Thank you," Claire quavered, her gaze shying away. Having Nicolas in her chamber while she was still abed made her feel more vulnerable than ever. Why had he come? She indicated a table. "She normally sets it there."

Nicolas deposited the tray, poured a cup and proffered it. Claire shifted the blankets so she could clutch them with one hand and still retain her modesty when she reached for the cup. She caught the twinkle in Nicolas's eyes, and knew he found amusement in her efforts.

"Did you sleep well?" he asked.

"Very well, thank you. And you?" She glanced at him from beneath her lashes, and sipped her chocolate.

"A most restful night," he replied.

"Mmm. So obviously the man on the beach didn't keep you up overlong." She peeked over the rim of her cup, satisfied at seeing him grow tense, and his eyes narrow.

"Pardon?"

"The man on the beach, Nicolas. Remember? What goes on? I fear I'm confused. You tell me not to go there, and yet you do. It's most odd. Every time I set foot out of this house, I find John trailing me—oh, ever so discreetly. And Nicolas, he carries a pistol. You carry one yourself, and I find that curious. You've been fighting, you've been shot and Lord knows what else has happened since I arrived. And if there are smugglers, I doubt they would bother me during the day."

"You cannot be too sure," Nicolas replied, shrugging. "I always maintain that it's better safe than sorry. Enjoy your chocolate, my love. I'll see you later, after breakfast."

He touched her brow with a gentle kiss, and turned, exiting the room in a trice. Claire stared after him, unable to muster a coherent thought. He'd called her his love. A tiny thrill leapt through her.

She lifted her chocolate with a light sigh, then frowned. He hadn't answered a single one of her questions.

"MAJOR," said Nicolas, slipping into the scullery. "I trust you slept well."

"As well as I might, Kenton," Robert answered around a mouthful of eggs. "And you?"

"Mmm," Nicolas grunted in reply. He flexed his wounded shoulder, peeked under his shirt and adjusted his bandage.

Robert watched him, a slow grin curling his lips. "Marriage sits well with you, I see. How's your wife?"

"Very well, thank you." Nicolas sat across from him at the scrubbed wooden table. Cook set a plate before him, and moved out of earshot, as did the potboy and maids. "Claire's becoming curious. Asking any number of questions about my doings. I'm not sure I can fob her off much longer without having to tell an out-and-out bouncer."

"Mmm," Robert responded around another mouthful. He sent Nicolas a sidelong glance. "Maybe she needs some diversion . . . to keep her mind off your activities."

"And what would you suggest?" Nicolas asked with deceptive mildness, refusing to rise to West's unspoken implication that Claire was bored with his company.

Robert paused, studied him a moment and shrugged. "Invite that termagant sister to stay . . . whatever is her name? Miss Katie? Kat's more like it. I vow she'll keep you both busy with that razor tongue of hers."

"I find Katie to be a pleasant young lady," Nicolas said in all sincerity.

Robert grunted. "She saw me the day after the, er, Park, with Pure Polly, you know," he explained. "Got the wrong impression. Knew I'd rendezvoused with Claire. Gave me a tongue-lashing I won't soon forget."

Nicolas chuckled. "Ah, of course she thought Polly was your paramour, and never would have guessed she was one of England's finest agents. Well, good for Miss Katie. You deserved it."

Robert gave him another grunt and a sharp glance. "So, do you invite her to stay?"

"It's a very good notion, West, I must say. Katie may be the perfect solution to my dilemma. I find her a practical and levelheaded girl. Doubtless she'll keep Claire busy and her nose out of mischief."

"And did Claire give you that wound?" Robert asked, wiping his mouth on a napkin. "Getting too friendly, eh?"

West's expression of bland amusement irked Nicolas. No matter how glad he was to see the man, he rather thought he'd like to wipe the smirk from the puppy's face. "You might say I've had some unwelcome visitors."

He quickly explained his night in the taproom and the subsequent shooting. "I've no choice but to confine both Claire and myself to the premises. It won't be long before they try again, and I'm not entirely certain I can fob Claire off with Banbury tales forever. However, there is a positive side to this. While they're engaged with me, you're free to get about finding Andrew. Any news in that area?"

"I suspect I'm getting closer. I've returned to inform you they killed the innkeeper. But before he died, he gave me brief descriptions of the men, so I thought I'd relay them to you, and perhaps you could let Renshaw start matching them to names."

Nicolas nodded. "Good. If they agree with my descriptions, mayhap it'll help Renshaw in his search. They're getting far too close for comfort. I don't like it."

"Nor do I. It's a tricky business, skulking about, never being sure you're asking questions of a safe person. I'm getting mightily sick of it all, Kenton. Do you know this is the first real meal I've taken in several days? I don't normally complain, but dash it, man, I've spent some damn hungry nights!''

Nicolas had the grace to feel compassion. ''I know. Can't be helped, I'm afraid. But you think you're getting closer?''

''I've had my eye on an ugly old washerwoman for days. I think she might have some information. If she becomes used to me she may let me talk to her. She's as skittery as an untried filly. I wouldn't have come back, but I really thought you ought to have those descriptions.'' He gave what information he had of the two men, describing them in close enough detail to satisfy Nicolas.

''I'd bet a monkey they're my taproom pair. You're doing well, West. Keep up the good work. With any luck, we'll have some men in irons before the month is out. I suggest you sleep all day and return tonight, unless, that is, you feel you need a greater rest?''

''Kind of you to be concerned, but no. Just ask Cook to make me a large package of good food.''

''It shall be done.'' Nicolas wasn't only satisfied, but excited by West's information—so much so that he offered his hand without compunction. West eyed him for a moment, and took it. A wry smile curved Nicolas's lips. ''Amazing what a common goal can do between enemies, eh, West?''

''I daresay we're more alike than we know, Kenton.''

Nicolas inclined his head, lifted a hand in salute and quit the room. He made directly for his study, there to pen a letter to Renshaw. Sealing it with wax, he began another: an invitation to Miss Katie Dempsey of Sussex, asking her to accept the hospitality of the Earl and

Countess of Kenton. And would she be pleased to return in the coach with the men and maid he sent with this missive?

His next order of business was to gather a retinue of menservants, and a maid as chaperon—in case the Dempseys couldn't spare one—and send them on their way to the next county. With Providence, Katie would arrive on the morrow, and keep his countess so busy that she would not have the time or the inclination to concern herself with his goings-on.

KATIE ARRIVED EARLY the next afternoon, ensconced in the Earl of Kenton's coach. She tumbled from the carriage with a footman's help, rushed up the stairs and into her sister's arms.

"Claire, dearest! It's so good to see you! I vow I've been nearly distracted now that you've gone. And did you see the procession which delivered me here? The townsfolk were agog at the entourage sent to escort me to see my sister, the countess!" She laughed and hugged Claire fiercely.

"Katie! How wonderful to see you!" Tears welled in Claire's eyes, and she laughed, squeezing her sister. "But how comes it that you're here? I knew nothing of this! I just happened to see the coach coming, and was curious as to who it might be!"

Katie laughed. "Your husband didn't tell you he invited me to visit? I make no doubt he wanted to surprise you! Wasn't that sweet of him? He's the most thoughtful of men, Claire. Why, he even sent one of your maids along for chaperon. The twins were green with envy that I was selected to visit, but Mama rather thought his lordship might have some rich and eligible gentlemen visiting, and that perhaps Nicolas was desirous of matchmaking. Isn't Mama silly?" She giggled, linking her arm with Claire's.

"How are Mama and the others?" Claire asked, wondering at this kindness of Nicolas's. Had he wanted to please her? She tightened her grip on Katie's arm, leading her into the house.

"We're all very well, and all send you their best." Katie fished in her reticule, bringing forth a letter. "This is from Mama. She apologizes for not writing sooner."

Claire accepted the missive, smiling at her mother's untidy scrawl. She tucked the treat into the pocket of her frock, intending to read it later. "I'm sorry to say we have no rich and eligible gentlemen in residence, but I do miss you all dreadfully."

"I didn't think for a moment that you did, and we've missed you, too. Why, I've been so bored, I've been reading those horrible gothic romances which Deirdre and Delight are so fond of. I vow those are the silliest stories! Why, one addlepated heroine is tapping at all the walls, searching for a secret tunnel, which, when she finds it, will put her life in the gravest danger! Now tell me, do you think that is sensible? And Deirdre and Delight will not hear a word of disparagement against them. What a lovely home! Do tell me you're happy here, Claire, and I won't prose on about how much we miss you!"

Claire laughed. "Yes, Katie, I daresay I'm very well. Nicolas is kind, and as you say, 'twas quite thoughtful of him to send for you." She didn't say so, but she wondered at his action. Why, he must have sent for Katie shortly after she'd asked him all those questions!

With dawning certainty, she realized she had asked him questions he did not want to answer. He *was* up to something... but what? A tunnel! Could that be how he got to and from the beach?

"Are you well, Claire?" Katie asked. "You've grown silent of a sudden."

"Yes, dear," was Claire's preoccupied reply. She came to a swift decision. "I daresay you'll want to wash. I'll ring for tea. I have something of import I must discuss with you."

Ten minutes later, Claire poured tea in the yellow salon. Katie, perched on her chair, waited with avid interest. Claire had some doubts about confiding her suspicions to her sister. Was it truly any of their business? But she was concerned, and the prospect of having a confidante proved too great a temptation. Besides, what if she were simply reading more into Nicolas's behaviour than was there?

"I'm waiting," said Katie as Claire took a dainty bite from a cucumber sandwich. "By the by, where is Nicolas?"

"He's closeted with his steward. He'll join us for dinner."

"Mmm. And so?"

"Katie, I vow he's up to something suspicious. The strangest things have been happening here." Claire shook her head, a frown creasing her brow. Leaning forward, she confided her doubts, finding it difficult to withhold any scrap of information that struck her as odd.

"Why would Nicolas warn me away from the beach, and then constantly stalk it himself? I begin to think he's a smuggler! I also believe there's a secret passageway somewhere in this house, lest how could he get down there so unobtrusively?"

"Claire, *you* haven't been reading those gothic romances? The Earl of Kenton a smuggler!"

"He's up to *something,* and I want to find out what it is."

"I would scarce credit this were it Deirdre or Delight telling me. But I can't believe you are become as fanciful as they." Katie frowned, considering her through narrowed eyes. "Yes, I daresay it would be fun to poke about, providing we do so discreetly. Where do you suppose this secret passageway is?"

"In the library, perhaps. Or his chamber. We'll look tomorrow, when Nicolas isn't about."

"Well, sister dear, you shan't find me poking about his chamber! So pray, don't even ask!" Katie giggled. "Well, I rather think I shan't be bored, even if you haven't a handsome gentleman in residence!"

CLAIRE CURLED into a ball on the overstuffed chair in her chamber. Emma had gone, leaving her clad in another flimsy gown, quite as pretty, and equally as daring as the previous. Claire no longer minded, thinking it unlikely that Nicolas would come to her. She knew some uneasiness at her failure to perform her wifely duties, and again wondered why Nicolas had left her so abruptly the other night.

She sighed, and cracked the seal on her mother's missive. "My dearest daughter," she read with a smile. Snuggling deeper into the chair, she perused the contents of the letter with slow delight, savouring every word. Lady Dempsey wrote how blessed they were by the marriage settlement "—why, Sir Percival looks ten years younger at being relieved of so great a burden!—" and how their lives were changing because of it.

Young Percy continued on at Eton, the girls had new frocks—before dinner, Katie had remarked she wouldn't need to borrow a single gown from Claire!—and Sir Percival had magnanimously conceded to allowing the front salon to be redecorated. A detailed account of colours and patterns was presented, and Claire became engrossed in the spirit of her mother's high expectations for their family.

Katie would be presented next year, and oh, how marvellous not to have to live another Season on a shoestring! There were even funds left to invest! And all because of the generosity of the Earl of Kenton. Her mother prayed Claire was happy in her new life, urged her to write and ended with a salutation to her new son—such a fine young man he was.

Claire refolded the letter and sat for a long time, tapping it against her chin. She could well imagine Sir Percival's lighthearted jubilation at his new good fortune, and conjured up his face with an easy smile upon his lips, the lines of strain erased from around his eyes. Her mother, too...no doubt she was the envy of her friends, and loving every moment of it, for having settled her first daughter so well.

As for Nicolas, he'd kept his end of the agreement, and more. He'd treated her kindly, opened his coffers for her use and had given her over and above what she could ever need. And she had yet to give him the one thing he'd asked of her: his heir.

She'd resented Nicolas, and the fact that she'd had to marry him while loving Robert. She'd clung to Robert like a talisman, using her love for him as an excuse not to make a full commitment to her marriage.

She frowned, contrite at her selfishness. Would it be so great a sacrifice, to surrender to Nicolas's kisses, to the warm strength of his arms about her? How onerous could it be? She needn't deny she enjoyed every slight touch he gave her.

She set aside the letter, gaining her feet in swift decision. The light folds of her nightgown swirling around her ankles gave her momentary pause, but she refused to permit her scanty attire to hinder her purpose. On legs quaking like jelly, she walked to the adjoining door, tapping a quick tattoo before her courage deserted her.

Nicolas's invitation to enter sounded surprised, and her resolve almost crumpled. He'd think her an addlepate, though, if she crept away, so quickly she opened the door, stepping inside. Closing the door softly, she sank back against it for support. Her heart beat with suffocating force, and she swallowed hard, realising her mouth had gone dry.

Nicolas's gaze roamed over his wife. Her beauty nearly took his breath away. He sat paralyzed on his bed, the covers drawn to his waist, his book falling forgotten to his side. He hoped she hadn't come to get her gown fastened, or some other such trivial thing, because if he touched her, he knew he wouldn't, nay couldn't, stop. He tore his eyes from her heaving chest, asking softly, "Yes, Claire?"

"My lord," she said, and stopped. She buried her hands in the shimmering folds of her gown, her gaze falling to her bare toes, and lifting again to his. "I, er, well, that is..." Her voice faded away, and green eyes pleaded with him for support.

Nicolas frowned, concerned now that her difficulty was greater than merely the need for a maid. He reached for his robe, pulling it across his back and pushing his arms through the sleeves. "Claire, I should hate to offend your sensibilities, so do look away for a moment."

She blushed, and immediately dropped her gaze. He slid out of bed and straightened the garment, tying the sash at his hips. Noting her intense discomfort, he padded to her on bare feet, and lifted her hand. "Mayhap you would feel more comfortable talking in your room?"

She gave a tiny nod. Nicolas tried to encourage her with a reassuring smile before opening the door and ushering her back through. Guiding her to a chair, he saw her seated and drew another close for himself. Then he leaned forward, taking both her hands in his. "Now, what is the problem? You aren't displeased that I sent for Katie?"

"Oh, no. No." Claire dragged her gaze from the V where his robe parted to display his handsome chest. "I'm most pleased to have Katie. Thank you."

Her tongue slid over dry lips, and she gulped in a deep breath. This was decidedly the most difficult task she'd ever undertaken. Her eyes lifted to his puzzled face. "She brought a letter from Mama."

"Oh? Are they faring well? None have taken ill?"

"Oh, no." She shook her head. "They are very well. Mama said they've been relieved of great financial burden, and Papa is looking near ten years younger!" She bit her bottom lip and plunged ahead. "Nicolas, you've fulfilled your part of the bargain. I only feel it right that I complete mine."

His face registered utter astonishment, and Claire rather suspected she'd actually disconcerted her composed, self-assured husband. A guarded expression crept across his features, suggesting a certain withdrawal. She remembered his comment about making love with a martyr, and feared that now she'd summoned her courage, he would refuse her. She couldn't let that happen, not after coming this far.

"I *want* to," she said in her strongest voice, tilting her chin just a fraction higher.

Nicolas held her honest green gaze for several long moments. He wasn't sure he could believe his ears. Claire coming to him willingly? No matter that it was only her sense of fairness which drove her on—would he be fool enough to reject her offering? God's teeth! He'd be the first to admit he wasn't an angel.

His eyes lowered, caressing the line of her jaw, the creamy smoothness of her throat, the teasing fullness of her breasts peeking impudently from beneath her transparent gown. His breath quivered through his nostrils, and he knew his control had come to an end. It was much more than the need of an heir which prompted his slow nod of acceptance.

He stood without a word, drawing her to her feet. His fingers glided through the silky mass of her hair to the back of her neck. Her face lifted, her lips tilted upwards. With a quiet groan, he claimed her mouth in a hot, searching kiss.

Scooping her up in his arms, he deposited her gently on the bed. Her flimsy lingerie skidded down her shoulder, her arm. One creamy breast, dipped in rose, gained freedom from its silky confines. Nicolas sought it with his mouth, and rather thought he was heaven bound.

CLAIRE STRETCHED her soft length along Nicolas's longer, harder, and ever so warm flesh. If a kitten felt like this, coddled, sassy and fulfilled, she made sure she was a kitten. She pushed her hair away from her face, daring to kiss Nicolas's collarbone, and then his neck.

Nicolas shivered, running a hand along her naked back. "Claire, kiss me again."

She smiled, knowing the utter freedom to touch another human in this warm, wonderful way. And she knew something else: her husband was made of passion and fire, and she loved it. She snuggled closer, lifting her head to gaze at him.

He smiled. "Well?"

A soft chuckle issued from her throat. "I only wonder," she murmured a trifle shyly, "why we waited so long."

Nicolas dragged a deep breath into his lungs. His lovemaking had pleased her! The knowledge heated him more than her silky, tender body. He remembered her eyes, clouded with desire, and her warm, welcoming softness. His heart pounded against his ribs like the sea against the shore. He embraced her, caressing her satiny flesh with a hand which trembled. Rolling her over, he poised above her, gazing down on her. He smoothed his thumb over her lips, resting it at the corner of her mouth.

"You're so beautiful, Claire," he murmured, his voice low and husky. "I've wanted to know you forever, and I assure you, 'twas well worth the wait."

Removing his thumb, he kissed the corner of her mouth. His lips played over the lushness of hers, his tongue dipped and teased. At her soft purr of encouragement, he deepened the kiss. He doubted he'd ever get enough of his lovely bride.

THE NEXT MORNING Katie sneezed over a dusty novel. "This is boring, Claire. I doubt there's such a thing as a secret passageway in this house. Really, I've let those horrid gothics go to my head!"

"Katie," said Claire. "I'm sure there's one somewhere in here!"

"That's all well and fine, Claire," responded Katie tartly, "but what if your husband finds us snooping in his library? How will we explain that away?"

"I told you, he won't catch us," said Claire, tapping at yet another panel. "He's helping train a young stallion, and I'm certain he'll be busy until lunch time, at least. Besides, we'll merely say we're searching for some

books on the subject of...well, I don't know...
something."

Katie pulled out a book, glancing at the title. "*The
Parliamentary History of England?*"

"Quick, Katie, look!" Claire pointed at a panel which
was sliding open. "I told you so!" she exclaimed triumphantly.

Katie scampered across the room, peering into the dark
cavern beyond. "Fancy that! We'll need a lantern."

They found the lantern and returned to the room,
touching the hidden latch again. The panel slid noise-
lessly aside, and they slipped through, trotting off down
the passageway with giggles of excitement. They followed it to the shore, to the scullery, and back to Nicolas's chamber. It was too fantastic to be true, thought
Claire. Nicolas using a secret means of removing to and
from the Strait? For what purpose? Did it have anything
to do with his need for an heir? A cold clutch of fear
gripped her, and she shook the feeling off, shuddering in
spite of herself.

CHAPTER ELEVEN

CLAIRE LAY in Nicolas's arms, content to rest with her ear on his chest, listening to the thud of his heart. One of his hands curled in her hair, the other about her waist. That she could find such sheer pleasure in his touch awed her. She recalled seeing his bedchamber in the town house, and the alarm that had skittered through her at the thought of being in just such a position as this with him. But now, amazingly enough, she found it a warm and wonderful haven, especially with the pouring rain battering on the roof and against the windowpanes.

Lovemaking, she mused, was more than merely pleasurable...it was quite wonderful, actually, if she were truthful. Nicolas was so sensitive, so gentle, but so passionate! The memory of his tenderness made her stomach constrict in a pleasant fashion. She did, however, know some guilt in that she had truly betrayed her love for Robert. It wasn't just that she'd married another man, and did her duty by him, but that she *liked* it.

Her thoughts rarely turned to Robert now, and that unsettled her. How could she love one man so much and forget him so quickly in the arms of another? Could it be that she didn't truly love Robert? The thought was too plaguey, so she shut her eyes and concentrated on the regular rhythm of Nicolas's heartbeat.

A scratching at the door interrupted her sleepy trance. Nicolas woke with a slight jerk, and gently eased away from her. Sad to have her warmth and pillow go, she curled into a tired ball and pretended to be asleep. He seized his robe and padded to the door.

Clark's low mumble met her ears, but she couldn't understand what he said. Nicolas grunted, shut the door and returned to the bed. She waited, hoping he'd crawl back in, but he didn't; instead he whispered, "Are you asleep, Claire?"

Her fatigue dissipated in an instant. She was sure he was up to something, and tonight would be her night to discover what it was. She decided not to answer, lying as still as possible, breathing deeply and slowly. She must have satisfied him, because without another sound, he turned and slipped silently out the door.

The door latch clicked shut. She threw her legs over the side of the bed and crossed to the wardrobe to find a quilted robe. The task was a trifle difficult in the dark, but within a minute, she wrapped the thick folds around her and shoved her feet into her slippers.

Peering out the door, she tiptoed down the hall, and slipped into Katie's room. Padding to the bed, she shook her sister. "Katie!" she whispered. "Wake up!"

"Hmm?" Katie mumbled sleepily. She sat up, coming alert. "Claire, what is it?"

"Nicolas sneaked out of the room tonight." She lifted Katie's robe off the end of the bed and tossed it to her. "Hurry, put this on! Tonight's our chance to find out what he's up to!"

"Claire, what if he catches us spying on him? Won't he be angry?" Katie asked, thrusting her arms into the robe and reaching for her slippers.

"He won't catch us. And if he does, well, I'm not afraid. He has no right to keep his nefarious goings-on from me. Clark's in on this. 'Tis he who aroused Nicolas from his bed.''

"Ooh, this grows more sinister by the moment. Your husband pays his servants to remain silent of his evil deeds. It must be something tremendous Claire," Katie continued, resuming a serious tone, "if he would take them into his confidence. Perhaps it would be best if we didn't interfere."

"Nonsense! If he can take a servant into his confidence, then why not his wife? I shan't tolerate such shabby treatment, Katie, I vow I shall not."

"You're right. I declare I'm beginning to dislike men more and more. They really are the most perfidious creatures. Unless, of course that's only true of the ones *you* attract."

"Hush, Katie, or I'll box your ears," Claire threatened in a whisper. Katie giggled. They slipped out her door and moved swiftly down the hall on silent feet.

"Where are we going?" Katie asked after several moments. Claire halted. "I don't know. Let's look for lights inside the house, and should we find none, we'll try the cave."

"Face the thieves in their den?" Katie gave a delicate shudder. "Onward, brave countess!"

Claire giggled and poked her sister in the ribs. Putting a finger to her lips, she slipped her arm through Katie's. They tiptoed down the stairs.

The house was perfectly still. No light burned in the library, none in any of the rooms on the upper level. They scuttled down the hall, but Katie's grip on her arm made Claire halt suddenly. She followed the direction in which Katie pointed, and saw a light coming from the scullery. Nodding, she held faster to her sister's arm, and they started off again. After descending the stairs in silence, they arranged themselves in a strategic position by the door, harking to the conversation within.

"You've found him, then," Nicolas said, excitement in his voice. "And he's alive?"

"Yes, but just barely, I understand," came a voice Claire recognised but couldn't immediately identify. It was tired and scratchy, and an underlying hint of weakness inflected its tone.

"Thank God!" Nicolas replied. "And the list?"

"I couldn't obtain it. I wasn't able to get that close. The washerwoman swore she hadn't seen any man, be he alive or dead. But I knew she had—I was sure of it—so I gave her the coin, asking if she did see him to give it to him, saying that help was on its way. I told her she'd be greatly rewarded for her efforts. She came back the next day, informing me he wasn't strong enough to travel alone, but she didn't offer the list. I judged that Andrew would know best whether to trust her with it—if he has it, that is."

Claire exchanged a puzzled glance with Katie, still unable to place the voice. She peered round the corner of the door. Her heart stopped. Could it be? Could that man, that dirty, unshaven, dark-haired, wet and bloody man, be her dashing Robert West? A gasp escaped her lips. Robert looked up, saw her and grimaced, sending a warning glance towards Nicolas.

Nicolas whirled on his heel, muttering something beneath his breath. "Claire!" His tone held distinct dismay. "What the devil are you doing here?"

She straightened into a more dignified stance, blushing now at being caught spying in so unladylike a manner. Grasping Katie's arm, she tugged her forward with her.

"But we're in our robes!" Katie whispered frantically.

"Pretend we're not" was Claire's low and urgent reply.

"Nicolas...Major West," she said, dismayed to hear the slight quaver in her voice. This would never do! She mustered her courage, clamping a firm hand on her unsettled emotions.

Holding her head higher, she swept into the room, saying in composed and commanding tones, "I might ask the same of you. If you haven't noticed, Major West is dripping blood and water all over Cook's polished floor. You haven't yet attended to his wound, but instead are blithering on about some man, some list and some washerwoman."

She glanced at the third party in the room. "Clark, fetch me some hot water and bandages. And I daresay we shall have a guest for at least a couple of nights, so do prepare him a room."

Robert glanced from Nicolas to her, and back to Nicolas. Fatigue and pained mockery lurked in his eyes. Claire looked at Nicolas, who spread his hands in a gesture of defeat.

"Do as my lady bids, Clark," he said, releasing the butler from his paralysis and sending him into motion. "I daresay Major West would be gratified to rest in a real bed."

The only response Robert gave was a lopsided grin.

"You might also ready a bath, Clark, and some fresh clothes. I daresay a razor wouldn't go amiss, either."

"Very good, m'lady," Clark said.

"No razor, Clark," interjected Nicolas. "But a bath is a must."

Claire cast her husband a curious glance, intrigued as to why he'd want Robert to save his beard.

Clark glanced from Nicolas to Claire. "Very good, m'lord, m'lady." He bustled from the room.

A tense, strained silence fell. Nicolas and Robert exchanged a glance which indicated their mutual conclusion that the fat was now in the fire. Claire watched them, wondering what she ought to do next.

Katie swept forward, breaking the heavy stillness. She moved towards the pot on the hearth, saying, "Well, one thing's certain, we can't allow Major West to bleed to death. I daresay that would set tongues to wagging, and we would be in a pretty mess, explaining it was his—*and* the Earl of Kenton's—smuggling activities which landed him in his predicament."

"Indeed," said Claire, moving towards the larder and bringing forth cheese and a cured ham. Her brain whirled. She suspected Nicolas and Robert would try to wheedle out of making confessions—but she wasn't going to let them, not now that she'd progressed this far. She eyed Nicolas.

"My lord, I rather think if you can't find your tongue, you might make yourself useful and find a bottle of wine. From the look of him, I would guess your visitor hasn't had a full meal in some days. You might utilise your time in the cellar to concoct a suitable tale for Katie and me. I suggest you make it a good one, for I doubt we'll believe you otherwise."

Nicolas and Robert groaned in unison, exchanging another glance and a grimace. Nicolas lifted a candle from the candelabrum on the table, and turned towards the wine cellar. He was back almost immediately, bearing a dusted bottle.

"I see you took your time selecting your best, Kenton," Robert mocked.

"All my wine is good" was Nicolas's curt reply.

"The finest from France, I'm sure" was Katie's tart interjection.

"Perhaps, Major," Claire said, "you might remove your shirt. It would be helpful if we could see the wound."

"I'm not a smuggler," Nicolas flatly denied.

"Your bandages and whatnot, my lady," Clark said, depositing his offerings on the table, along with a decanter of brandy. He went to the fire, added two more pieces of wood and lifted a larger kettle of water to the hook. He bowed out of the scullery, mumbling something about preparing the room.

"I daresay it wouldn't be improper for me to bare my chest to you, m'lady, your being married and all," Robert teased, "but I imagine your sister might be offended by the sight."

"I rather think not," said Katie, her tones just shy of a snap. "You puff up your consequence too much. Your chest is a matter of indifference to me, be it bare or be it clothed."

Nicolas made a noise which sounded suspiciously like a strangled chuckle.

"Very well," Robert rallied, shrugging out of the garment. "I was merely concerned for your sensibilities, but I see you have none."

Katie plopped a bowl of warm water on the table, mindless of the waves which splashed over the sides. "Have a care, Major," she warned. "I would take a certain satisfaction in giving you a well-needed bath just now."

"Odso," Robert growled. "Well, I wouldn't deny myself the pleasure of a harem girl, if that's what you're offering."

Katie picked up the bowl of water and dumped it over his head.

"Oh, for pity's sake!" Claire jumped back, liberally doused herself. She looked from a steaming Katie to a drenched Robert. The two glared daggers at each other. Nicolas had the audacity to burst into laughter, and she couldn't help but join him.

"He insults me," Katie sputtered, glaring at Nicolas, "and you can do nothing but laugh?"

Nicolas sobered, though a smile still lurked on his lips and in his eyes. "You've done a fine job handling him, Katie. I see no reason why I should interfere."

"In the meantime," muttered Robert, lifting a towel from the table and dabbing at his face, "I stand in danger of dying before your eyes. Really, Kenton, I expected better treatment in your home. Or was it your intention to set Kat upon me?"

"My name is Katie, sir," said Katie, "and I will thank you to remember it."

"Ah, but Kat suits you much better," Robert said with a mocking grin.

Katie glared at him.

"You might have a care for your hide, West," Nicolas drawled in an amused tone. "I believe Katie will be helping to nurse you. I'd be sweeter to her, were I you."

"You may have a point there, old man. Well, Miss Katie, are you going to replace the water you dumped on my head, or are you going to stand there slaying me with your eyes? I'd like to eat something soon, if you don't mind."

With a sniff, Katie picked up the bowl and flounced to the hearth.

"If you're not a smuggler, Nicolas," Claire said, "what are you? A wounded Robert West is the last person I'd expect to grace your kitchen. Have you thought up a pretty story, or must I wait longer for an explanation?" She sounded sweet, even innocent, but within she seethed with curiosity. What the devil were they about?

"Well, you see . . ." began Nicolas, and stopped.

"It's all very mundane . . ." began Robert, and stopped. After a moment, when Nicolas didn't speak, he said, "Nicolas and I are chance acquai—"

Even as Nicolas said, "Robert and I are old—"

Both men clamped their lips together.

"Rubbish!" Claire snapped. She straightened from inspecting Robert's wound and stared her husband full in the face. "I will not be fobbed off with Banbury tales. There is a reason, Nicolas, why you have a secret passage running to a cave on the beach, a reason why Robert knows of it, and a reason why he's now sitting here with a gash in his shoulder, which was made by a bullet, if I'm not mistaken. Now, if you aren't smuggling illicit goods from France, pray tell, what *are* you doing?"

Nicolas sighed and availed himself of a chair. He exchanged another glance with Robert, who shrugged unhelpfully. Lifting a piece of gauze bandaging, he rolled it round and round. The abstracted gesture reminded Claire of how he'd twined her hair round his fingers the night they'd met in Hyde Park. He was evidently thinking deeply.

Katie returned with the water, but Claire made no move to tend the wound. She wasn't about to remove her pointed stare from Nicolas. Katie lifted a towel from Clark's assortment and dipped it in the bowl.

"Have a care, Kat," Robert drawled. "I am rather attached to my hide."

"Obviously you are not, or you wouldn't call me 'Kat,'" Katie retorted. She gently dabbed the wound, rinsed the cloth and dabbed again.

"The work Major West and I are involved in is highly confidential," Nicolas finally murmured, returning the direct challenge in Claire's eyes.

"Claire and I won't tell," Katie said. "We already know you're in league with Major West. We also know it concerns a man, a coin, a washerwoman and a list. I'm sure we shouldn't breathe a word—not, that is, if we knew the truth of the matter."

"Is that a threat, Miss Katie?" Robert asked. "What should you do if we didn't choose to tell the truth?"

"Well, I daresay, as concerned citizens and loyal subjects of our King, we should have no recourse but to bring this matter before the proper authorities."

"A woman can't testify against her husband," West pointed out with silky assurance.

Katie made a grim smile. "I can testify against *you*."

"Marry me, my heart?"

She scrubbed his wound hard, and he howled.

Claire watched Nicolas, a shard of fear piercing the soft peace she'd gained a short time ago, lying in his arms. Could he truly be a smuggler, and yet love her with such tenderness?

"Nicolas?" His name was a whispered plea.

She gazed into his grey eyes which were narrowed in thought. Nicolas's features softened, his eyes lost their guarded look, and he shrugged. "We're spies."

Claire found herself bereft of words.

"Good or bad?" Katie asked noncommittally. "Do you work for England or France?"

"England, of course," Robert replied. Katie probed deeper into the wound and he ground his teeth.

"I think," Claire murmured, only a trifle relieved, "that you should pour the wine, Nicolas. This may be a rather lengthy explanation."

Robert groaned through clenched teeth. "I'll take brandy, if it's all the same to you. Dash it all, m'dear, aren't you yet satisfied that it's clean?"

"Brandy would be good, Claire," Katie said. "We need something to disinfect this wound. You'll have to bandage it, too, as I haven't a notion how to do so."

Claire placed a glass in Robert's hand and soaked a cloth in the brew. Slowly she wrung it out over Robert's wound. She remembered performing much the same operation on Nicolas, and though she knew sympathy for Robert's pain, somehow, in some way, she didn't experience the same tug of emotion she had felt while attending Nicolas—nor the horrible fear that he might have been killed.

"So, Major West," she said, "you were in France spying and almost caught a bullet for your efforts. Is that it?"

"Something like that."

She applied the bandage, conscious of Robert's intense scrutiny. She didn't dare look at him, knowing Nicolas watched them. She did notice, however, that though Robert's physique was attractive, it wasn't nearly so handsome as Nicolas's. Her husband's body seemed so much more warm...and approachable. Precisely like Nicolas himself, once you came to know him. The realisation surprised her, and an involuntary warmth seeped through her. She dared not glance at her husband, so leaned closer in to her work.

Nicolas took up a knife and sliced the ham and cheese. "Have we any bread, Katie? Claire, are you quite done with that bandage? Major West is sure to become tired of all this fussing."

"Not at all," Robert teased, flashing a sardonic grin, and flicking his blue eyes over Claire's face. "I've never had such lovely angels to attend me. I shan't utter a word of complaint."

Claire ignored both Robert's teasing and Nicolas's fierce frown. After a final adjustment and pat to her work, she turned to her husband, her eyes snapping. "I'm quite done, my lord. Now perhaps you might call halt to your delaying tactics and enlighten us."

His grey gaze locked with hers, and she refused to shy away. He had no right to be short with her. He lifted one shoulder in a tiny shrug and took a chair. Pushing some food towards Robert, who gladly availed himself of the offering, he prepared himself a meal of cheese heaped on ham heaped on bread.

Claire rolled a piece of ham around a slice of cheese and waited. Katie, sipping her wine, raised an enquiring brow.

Nicolas swallowed and drank from his wine. "Andrew Marsh, Lord Rutledge, is the man we spoke of." He made a quick recounting of a tale of traitors, a missing agent, and the all-important list, finishing with: "Robert has managed to locate Andrew, and now we must needs decide how best to bring him back to English soil, with his list of names—and his life—intact."

Claire frowned and sipped thoughtfully at her wine. Though her mind was clearer on certain facts, her heart wasn't set to rest. If anything, it pulsed with more turmoil. Nicolas hadn't said it, but their quest to return Lord Rutledge to England was fraught with danger. He'd also neglected to mention his own wound, and the fact that it hadn't been an accident. She lifted her gaze to her husband. "Someone is trying to kill you."

Nicolas nodded slowly. "Which is why Major West was assigned the task of locating Andrew. The men we seek learned my description, making it unsafe for me to return to France."

"And hardly safe to stay in England," she mused. No wonder he'd made such haste to marry. It wasn't greatly flattering that he'd chosen her for the sole purpose of securing his line, but she now understood his urgency. Still, she thought it beastly of Nicolas to marry her, knowing full well he might leave her a widow in undue haste. Her heart constricted into a tight, painful knot. *What if he were killed?*

The thought overwhelmed her. She needed a haven to sort out her feelings. Rising hastily from the table, she clasped her hands together to still their sudden trembling. "I rather think I shall retire now. Major West, try not to wet your bandages whilst you bathe. Nicolas, perhaps you might find Clark and see your guest settled. Come along, Katie. Good night, gentlemen."

CLAIRE BURROWED DEEPER into the covers, warding off an unpleasant chill. Instead of finding satisfaction in knowing the answers to her questions, she rather desired ignorance. True, all Nicolas's strange actions made perfect sense now—his haste to take a wife, his need for an heir—but 'twas small consolation in light of the knowledge she'd just gleaned. His life was in danger: someone wanted him dead, and would likely stop at nothing to see that goal accomplished.

Filthy murderers! She shivered again, and wished Nicolas might come to her, to warm her with his presence.

Thank God he wouldn't be returning to France! At least at Kenwood Park he knew a modicum of safety. Her brow wrinkled in thought. Why did she feel such intense concern for the man she hadn't wanted to marry?

Her emotions regarding her husband, she acknowledged, had undergone a radical change. Did she love him? The question posed itself as stealthily as a stalking cat. No, she quickly decided . . . at least, she didn't *think* so. After all, 'twas only natural to feel concern for his safety—she *was* his wife.

Then why was she oddly thankful Robert would return to France, and not Nicolas? Not that she liked to see Robert go, either, but his departure was clearly the lesser of two evils. Though Robert was the man she professed to love, her heart hadn't fluttered when she'd seen him tonight, when she'd touched him. The rapture she'd once known at being in his presence, at feeling blue eyes caress her face, his teasing grin lifting her heart, wasn't there.

In the darkness of her chamber, she finally admitted that Robert West no longer held her heart. She'd been infatuated with his good looks, and flattered by his attentions . . . but she didn't love him. Releasing the bonds of the true love she'd imagined between them was quite painless, even rather effortless. In fact, it was a relief to realise her heart belonged to no one.

And she'd best keep it that way. Nicolas desired no affection from his wife, and wanted to give none. She'd be a fool to toss her heart in that direction . . . *if she hadn't already.*

THE NEXT MORNING, Claire made her way to the drawing-room, hoping to find the other members of the household there. Nicolas hadn't returned to her last night, and neither had he visited this morning. Was he angry that she'd tended Robert? He had been rather tense, and even short, but why? Especially when he viewed her as little more than the means of obtaining an heir. She stepped inside the drawing-room, finding Robert its sole occupant.

"Good morning, Claire." He uncoiled himself from his chair and rose. Lifting her hand, he pressed a respectful kiss on the back of it.

"Good morning, Robert," Claire returned with a smile, knowing a satisfying ease in his presence. "You look much improved, though I must say your attire seems somewhat ill suited to all that hair on your face."

Robert chuckled. "Indeed. Just one plaguey nuisance of being a military man. Makes it damnably difficult to charm the ladies."

Claire laughed. "Indeed. How is your shoulder?"

"A bloody bother, but better. I mend quickly." An engaging grin lit his face, and he offered his arm. "It's a beautiful day. Might we take a stroll?"

"Certainly." Claire, happy for the opportunity of his company, took his arm. Though she knew now she did not love him, she did like Robert; his grin was so infectious. They walked in companionable silence down the wide steps and into the manicured gardens beyond.

Robert picked a bloom, and with a sweeping bow, offered it to her. "I neglected to say how lovely you look today, m'lady. My apologies. It seems the country, and marriage, suit you admirably. I daresay you're fairer now than when I last saw you in London."

"Thank you, Robert," she responded. "I am content."

"Kenton treats you well?"

"He's most kind."

"So you've fallen in love with him, eh,?"

"Of course I have not! What a buffleheaded thing to say. Ours is a marriage of convenience. Are you quite sure you didn't take a knock to the head, as well? You must know why Nicolas married me." Not for a moment would she consider whether his words carried a whisper of truth.

"Mmm. He's in love with you."

She glanced sharply at him. Nicolas—in love with her? She quashed a tiny leap of joy, knowing it was impossible, and utter foolishness for her to hope as much. "Fustian! You have windmills in your head. Now I'm *convinced* something has happened to your powers of reasoning. He merely needs an heir."

"Oh, I'm aware of that. But I rather suspect—no, more than suspect, I *know* he married you for another reason, as well." He gave her a cursory glance. "He loves you."

"Robert, I can scarce credit I'm hearing this! Nicolas does not love me, so do stop your prattling!" Did Robert see something she didn't? Would it be the height of idiocy to entertain the hope that Nicolas regarded her in a warmer light than she suspected?

Robert flashed a brilliant smile, and seated himself on a nearby bench, drawing her down beside him. "I would like to say 'Methinks the lady doth protest too much,' but I won't. I shan't tease you with it any longer. After all, you must know better than I, and if you say it isn't so, then it isn't."

Claire accepted his words without comment, knowing he wasn't convinced that she and Nicolas weren't in love with each other. Nicolas had made it perfectly clear that he wanted none of her affection, but she didn't like confessing as much to Robert. She hastened to change the subject.

"You are different, Robert. You seem more... mature."

"Running for his life will do that to a man. You've changed, too."

Claire laughed. "Marriage will do that to a woman. When did you discover you must needs go to France?"

Robert snorted, shaking his head. "The day after I asked you to elope with me." He reached for her hand. "I owe you an apology, Claire. At the time, I was irritated that Kenton had the audacity to approach you when he knew his life was in danger. He'd nearly been killed three times before getting out of France, and I knew it wouldn't be long before our traitors located him in England." He grimaced. "I thought I would, under the circumstances, make a better husband. Little did I know that I'd been commissioned for the job of finding Andrew. I might have guessed it, though, having done the preliminary investigations into the attacks on Kenton's life."

He lifted one shoulder in a conceding gesture. "It was the height of foolishness for me to think I could take a wife. I had... have nothing to offer. Though I hope it won't happen, if you are left Kenton's widow, at least you'll be wealthy. I'm sorry... not only for asking for you to elope with me, but also for the danger in which I placed your reputation. As your young sister, Katie, pointed out to me, it was a dashed beastly thing to ask of you."

"Katie said that?"

"She did, and very heatedly, I might add. She's a regular virago when she puts her mind to it. Methinks she has little love for me." He chuckled. "And I for her."

Claire grew silent, her brow furrowed in thought. Robert's handsome apology was gratifying to receive, but the thought of becoming Nicolas's widow made her physically ill. He hadn't mentioned the attempts on his life last night. And yet he'd married her, knowing it possible he might never see his son, should she have the good fortune to conceive. She didn't know which bothered her more—that she might be left a widow or that he'd known full well that he might be killed. Her heart contracted, tears pricked her eyes, coming close to spilling over.

"Excuse me, Major West. I must see to the menus."

He stood immediately and reached for her hand. "One moment, Claire. I must tell you that I wish you very happy with Nicolas. I think we both know now we wouldn't have suited."

His voice, soft, gentle, pleaded for understanding. Claire gave it, relieved she hadn't broken his heart. She nodded, and even mustered a smile. "Thank you, Robert." She forced the words past the lump in her throat, and sought to quell her tears. Lifting on tiptoe, she grazed his cheek with a quick kiss. "I'm happy we're in agreement on that subject."

Withdrawing her hand from his, she picked up her skirts, and walked to the house with as much haste as graceful deportment allowed. She couldn't let him see how the thought of losing Nicolas tore at her. She forbade the tears to fall until she was safely in her chamber.

CHAPTER TWELVE

NICOLAS SAT at the desk in his study, staring grimly out the window and into the garden beyond. The sight of Claire, with her hand on Robert's arm, had a decidedly unpleasant effect on his temper. He wanted to throttle Robert West for having the audacity to speak with her, and he wanted to shake Claire for having the temerity to seek out the man's presence.

He hadn't liked her attending West last night—not a bit. In fact, he'd thought he might choke West for having the gall to be alive! And there he was, doing the pretty, flirting with Claire, bowing and offering a fresh bloom. Nicolas wanted to strangle him. The smile Claire tilted up at West only gave Nicolas more cause to grind his teeth. She obviously hadn't surrendered her love for the man.

But why, after all, should he care? And, blast it, he *did* care! Why? What did it matter? He sighed. He loved her, that was why. The sudden knowledge didn't startle him; it seemed he'd known it forever. He cradled his head in his hands, wondering why on earth he hadn't realised it before.

He'd loved her from the beginning, from the first time he'd seen her standing across Lady Hathaway's ballroom. He loved her beauty, her smile, her honesty, her entire being. He loved Claire—the soft sweetness of her melting in his arms, the feel of her lips clinging to his.

Possessing her body wasn't enough. He wanted all of her. Had she dreamed of Robert West when she lay in his arms? Nicolas smote one fist into the other palm. Damn! He lifted his quill, tapping the tip against a piece of paper.

He'd said he cared nought for affection. What a fool he'd been! In truth, he wanted to be loved for himself, not for what he could give. And he'd run from love because he'd never thought he could receive it. The black irony was that he'd fallen in love with a woman who wanted nothing from him, one whose heart already belonged to another.

Claire must know Robert had to return to France. Nicolas had yet to inform her that he would go with West. Andrew needed two men to carry him out, and they must move with all haste lest they risk detection. Would any of them return alive?

Nicolas gazed out the window, saw Claire stand, saw West rise and catch her hand. There was an exchange of words, and she kissed him on the cheek. Nicolas sucked air into his lungs. Claire turned, coming towards the house, looking decidedly weepy. What had West said? That lout! He'd box his ears! He rose from the desk and went to the door, opening it in time to see Claire sweep up the stairs and towards her chamber.

He followed her and knocked tentatively on her door, opening it to find her in tears. She turned away from him, and he felt as if a knife was being twisted in him. Loving her was one thing, but knowing that he loved her was quite another. He steeled himself for rejection, and walked to her, placing his hands gently on her arms.

"Claire," he said, her name but a whisper on his lips.

Claire turned into Nicolas's arms, unable to resist the comfort he offered. She leaned into his strong, support-

ing chest and allowed her tears free rein. She treasured
having him close, warm and alive. After some minutes,
she lifted her head. "Nicolas."

"Claire, don't weep any more," he whispered.
"Please, say you won't."

Her lashes fluttered up, and she studied him for the
first time that morning. Her eyes narrowed. "You
haven't shaved." The statement sounded like an accusa-
tion even to her ears.

Nicolas closed his eyes in a brief, defeated gesture. "I
have to return to France with Major West."

She struggled out of his arms, and stared hard at him.
"But... but they shot him! They've shot you! Nicolas—
no!"

"I have no choice, Claire."

She gasped for air, her head reeling. "Your life is in
danger there."

"My life is in danger everywhere. Robert can't accomplish the task alone. Andrew is too weak, and two
healthy men can move him faster than one. I must help
bring Andrew out. If we return alive, I'll be able to live
peacefully, without looking over my shoulder forever."

"And if you don't return alive?"

"Well, should that be the case, I daresay I'll not have
to worry about guarding my backside, either. It's the only
way, Claire. As long as these traitors are about, we'll
never be safe and free."

He smoothed his hand over her tummy, for a moment, looking sad and pensive. His gaze met hers, full of
an emotion she'd never seen in their clear grey depths.
Love? Could Robert possibly have been correct?

"And our child, should we have one, will be safe to
grow." His eyes pleaded for understanding. "I must go."

Claire pushed away from him. "You are a fiend, Nicolas Shea. You married me, knowing full well you might leave me a widow. I know you needed an heir, but I didn't know he might never see his father! Leave my chamber—at once!"

Nicolas sighed, deeply and heavily. He gazed at her, stepped towards her and stopped. "I'm sorry."

Claire pointed towards the connecting door. She couldn't surrender . . . her emotions were too ravaged.

Nicolas stepped through the door, closing it quietly behind him. Claire stared at it for long moments. Her knees buckled under her and she sank to the floor, bowing her head. Tears fell in silent testimony of her grief.

NICOLAS BECAME a bit shaggier about the face in the next two days. Claire had to admit the stubble rather suited him, lending him a rakish quality she hadn't heretofore associated with him. That he appeared more powerfully attractive was all very well, but his growing hair only served to remind her of the threatening prospect of living life without him.

Perhaps a short month ago, she might have been pleased if he had disappeared from the face of the earth, but now, somehow, her spirit became morose and melancholic at the thought of his being wrenched from her side. Still, she wasn't inclined to speak to him. Oh, of a surety, she was polite, insofar as she had to be. And Nicolas hadn't visited her room once since she asked him—nay, commanded him—to leave.

She was a bundle of pent-up emotion. Nicolas and Robert spent many hours in his study, plotting their every move to get Andrew out efficiently and speedily. Knowing they also calculated their possible demise didn't soothe Claire's nerves one whit.

Even Robert failed to lift her spirits. But his and Katie's spats were diverting, and allowed her to maintain a semblance of good humour... until Nicolas announced at lunch that he and Robert would return to France at dusk. Claire's spoon froze halfway to her mouth. Her gaze flew to his, then fell to her plate.

"I must ask for your promise, ladies, that you won't leave the garden," Nicolas continued with firm emphasis. "It's imperative, for your own safety, that you stay close so the servants can protect you. We don't know with whom we're dealing. If they know we've found Andrew and the list, there's no telling what they might do to protect themselves. Do I have your word?"

Claire didn't have the heart to disagree, and nodded in unison with Katie.

"Good," he said. "I've written to my superior, Lord Renshaw. I daresay he may pay you a visit in a day or two."

"When may we expect your return?" asked Katie.

"God willing, we could be back in as little as thirty-two hours," Nicolas replied.

He and Robert had apparently mapped their plans down to the very minute. The knowledge didn't decrease Claire's ever-growing fear.

At dusk, Nicolas enfolded her hands in his. His eyes held a hint of sadness. "Claire, if you bear our child, you won't speak ill of me to him?"

A sudden, powerful constriction in her throat rendered her unable to speak. She shook her head, knowing her eyes were wide with unshed tears.

"Goodbye, Claire," he murmured softly, his eyes eloquent with tenderness. He placed a gentle kiss on her mouth and turned away.

"God speed, Nicolas," she whispered, forcing the words past the lump in her throat. The desire to throw her arms about him and beg him not to go increased, but her dignity, and the knowledge of his sense of duty, forbade her.

She watched him and Robert depart, staring at his back until he disappeared from her view.

THIRTY-TWO HOURS seemed a lifetime of agony and anxiety to Claire. She'd tried to sleep, she'd tried to eat, she'd even tried tending her herb garden—all with the same result: failure. She'd spent more time in the drawing-room, gazing out the French doors to the waters beyond.

"Claire, dearest, you've been staring outside this past age! It's four in the morning, and ever so dark. Can you not come and share a dish of tea with me?" Katie asked, her voice gentle.

Claire turned from the window, her fingers pleating the folds of her gown. "Katie, I vow I couldn't drink a drop! They're due back, and...and what if he doesn't return?" Her voice ended in a whisper, and she flicked at the tears spilling from her eyes.

Katie frowned in sympathy, moving forward to take Claire's hands in hers. "Oh, dearest! How awful for you. I can't claim to have been in love, but I see how it affects you, and it breaks my heart to see you so. I wish I could assure you that they'll return, but we both know how empty those words would be. However, for your sake, Claire, I do hope Robert doesn't die."

Claire gave her a sharp glance. *Robert?* Why she'd scarcely given him a thought. No, 'twas Nicolas...*Nicolas!* "No, Katie," she averred, "it's not Robert.

It's Nicolas. If he doesn't return—oh, Katie! I shall truly want to die!''

"Nicolas?" Katie queried, her brow puckered in a frown. "But I thought . . ."

"I've been such a paper skull!" Claire pressed her fingers to her temples, her tears coursing down in abandon. She grasped the handerkerchief Katie stuffed into her hand. "I love Nicolas, though I didn't realize how much until now. I hardly spoke to him for two whole days, and I can scarcely credit I was so pig-headed and stupid not to love him every moment I had to spend with him, and now he's gone and he may never return! Oh, Katie, what if I never get to tell him I think he's the most wonderful man alive, the most sweet, sensitive and loving man I've ever met! And that I'm so glad he married me, and so thankful I grew to know him.

"He asked me not to speak ill of him to our child, should I have one. Oh, I know he doesn't think he'll come back, and if he doesn't think so, then I have no hope!" Another bout of tears burst forth and she buried her face in the handkerchief.

"Oh, Claire, how awful!" Katie cried, her voice choked with emotion. She wrapped her arms about her sister, and gave way to her own flood of tears.

They cried together for some minutes.

"Well," said Claire with a sniffle, "'tis clear we aren't doing much good by sitting here weeping. If they're coming, they should be here soon. I intend to gather some pistols and go through to the cave, and I shall be there if he needs me."

"Claire! Nicolas left strict instructions! You mustn't disobey him."

"If he dies, sister," Claire returned with a tilt of her head and a stubborn jut of her chin, "how will he ever know I disobeyed him? Besides, I can't bear to sit here useless, when he may be in forfeit of his life.'' Her voice strengthened in her determination. ''You may obey him if you like, but I shall find a brace of pistols, and wait for him in the cave . . . should he return, that is.''

Katie spread her hands in helpless indecision. She chewed her bottom lip, considering her sister with some unease. Finally, she shrugged. ''Very well, Claire, I'll go with you, but if Nicolas does live to learn of it, I vow you'd better take his tongue-lashing, not I!''

NICOLAS HAD NEVER MADE a journey more fraught with tension—not that he'd expected a picnic. That ugly little washerwoman had *insisted* on returning with them, going so far as to shove his pouch of gold back at him with a volley of French curses. She didn't want his money, she wanted passage to England. Only Andrew's assertion that he owed her his life bent Nicolas's decision in her favour. To her credit, and considering her advanced years, she was spry.

Getting Andrew to the boat had required nothing short of a miracle, what with the man nearly dead from emaciation, and weak as a newborn kitten. He and Robert almost had to carry him, all the while looking over their shoulders, knowing they'd attracted attention—how could they not?—and that their attackers might not be far behind.

No sooner had Andrew toppled into the boat than his weapon had fallen out, rapidly sinking into the murky depths. A cold drizzle increased their discomfort, and the Strait, in one of its mercurial moods, was rough and choppy. Propelling their craft through the water was a battle. And one more person, however light she'd assured them she was, merely added to their burden.

Every fibre of Nicolas's body protested loudly with fatigue. Robert wasn't in any better shape, and Andrew... well, Andrew was doing damn well just to sit straight. But his spirits were high, and he'd vowed earlier that escaping France had made him a new man. He'd found the food basket Cook had sent, and now munched contentedly on a chicken leg.

Nicolas envied Andrew his lack of concern. But he deserved it, poor soul. And Nicolas was only too thankful to have his friend in company, and to be making, at last, for England. However, he had an unsettling premonition that all was not well. Something sinister seemed to be rolling towards them on the waves. He pulled hard at his oar, keeping an ever alert eye on the inky darkness.

Five more miles, five more miles, he told his aching arms, his heaving chest. They'd been rowing for hours. Surely England couldn't be much farther. He and Robert were well matched at the oars. Both were strong, and dipped their oars with a sureness and grace in exact precision. A little more than an hour, and they should be home.

The minutes ticked by, each one bringing them ever closer to safety, ever closer to flexing his aching muscles, and ever closer to Claire. He wanted to hold her. He hoped she'd let him. He'd scarcely thought of anything else since their leavetaking. The expression in her eyes, sad and frightened, continued to haunt him.

A loud crack reverberated through the night. All three men jumped with a sudden, tense watchfulness.

"Merde!" exclaimed the washerwoman.

More cracks, and a volley of shots splattered into the water about their craft, falling so close as to make the men mutter their own round curses.

"Hell and damnation!" Robert's oath roared above the howl of the wind. "They're on our tail! Can you see them? They aren't thirty yards back!"

Nicolas saw them clearly enough. Noisy shots challenged the wind for supremacy, and water splashed just feet away. "Blast and damn!" he growled in turn, reaching inside his coat for his pistol. "Ready your weapon, West!" he shouted. "And keep rowing! Don't shoot unless you have to. Veer right!"

"Nicolas," Andrew's fatigued voice rose above the din. "I'm putting the list in your waistband. If the boat gets hit, don't worry about me. Give me your word you'll get yourself to shore."

"We'll all make it to shore," Nicolas promised grimly, laying the pistol on his lap and setting every ounce of his brawn into the oar.

"And if we don't," came Andrew's reply, as he tucked the list, secured in a leather pouch, inside Nicolas's waistband, "you must promise to leave me to fend for myself. Recall your duty to your country...and your new bride."

A vision of Claire danced from the water's spray, and Nicolas grimaced with a pain that erupted from the heart. "I'll do my best, old man. That's all I can promise."

"They're gaining on us!" Robert shouted. A ball hit the water beside him. "Damn, that almost hit my oar!"

Nicolas cursed the night, the rough waters, their attackers and the miles left to shore. "Veer left! We'll try to keep away from their bullets, and to expend none of our own."

"They must have an arsenal with them!" Robert returned. "I've counted twelve shots! Are you sure there's only two of them?"

"There must be three!" Now that he gave thought to it, the number seemed logical. Three...or more. How else could they be gaining and still have hands left to fire? The only advice he could give West was "Row *harder!*"

"I'm rowing as hard as I can!" Robert growled. "Blast this damned storm!"

"This damned storm is saving us!" Nicolas roared back. "If they could see us, we'd be dead. We're outgunned, as sure as I'm sitting here!"

Andrew pulled himself up and grasped the pistol on Nicolas's lap. "I'll give those bastards something to chew on!" he muttered, taking aim.

"Just don't shoot our boat," Robert groaned, warily eyeing Andrew's weak grip.

Andrew pulled the trigger, the blast knocking him sideways.

"Give me that damn pistol!" said the washerwoman in crystal-clear English.

Nicolas was surprised not only by her grasp of the language, but the strength of her voice. My God! They hadn't taken a traitor on board with them? He glanced swiftly about, relieved to see the ugly little woman taking straight aim at their attackers. Her finger squeezed the trigger, accompanied with her bellow, "Take that, you *swine!*"

Nicolas gulped back a chuckle. Who *was* this French creature? So long as she was on their side, he supposed it didn't matter.

"We can't be more than a mile to shore!" he shouted in encouragement. A mile, give or take a few. One more mile...but would it save them?

"Good," Robert declared. "My arms would like to fall off!"

"And mine," agreed Nicolas. A ball crashed in the water beside him and he flinched, wondering when one would hit its mark and smash into their craft, or worse yet, one of them. "They're closing in, West! Let's give it all we've got!"

Both men put every ounce of their strength into the oars, each herculean effort bringing them nearer, ever nearer the shore.

"We're making it, men!" Andrew shouted. "I can see the beach, not fifty feet away."

"And a damn good thing," Robert growled. The water splashed beside him, giving evidence to another ball meeting a wet grave.

Nicolas knew that even if they made it, they wouldn't get safely inside the cave and up the passage. They were off course by at least fifty yards. Though the small percentage of error was a credit to their skills, it would in no wise save their lives. Their small supply of bullets was already dangerously low; he'd counted four shots from the washerwoman. Unless they killed their men, it was doubtful they'd make it to the safety of the house. Deadly lead whizzed past his head, and he grimaced.

"Use your weapon, West!"

Robert grasped his pistol, sending a shot across the water. The firing ceased. "Got their shooter, be hanged if I didn't!" he shouted triumphantly.

He rose a trifle, peering into the blackness and taking careful aim. Another pistol cracked. With a grunt of surprise and pain, Robert toppled into the water, taking his pistol with him.

Nicolas grasped the tragedy in an instant. Good God, Robert had been hit! The shore but five yards away, and their pursuers not more than twenty. Could he rescue Robert and still make it to shore with Andrew? What about the list? They'd all be killed. But if he came back alive, and West didn't, Claire would never forgive him.

"Take an oar, Andrew!" he yelled, and dived into the water.

"Mon Dieu!" The washerwoman grabbed both oars.

Robert valiantly treaded water, using one arm. "Kenton," he groaned, "it's my shoulder. 'Tis useless. Blast it, man, why'd you come after me? What the hell are you about?"

"Shut your trap, West, and put your good arm around my shoulder. Damn if I'll give up now when we've come this far!"

"You've apartments to let, Kenton," Robert grated, nevertheless obeying him. Nicolas swam beside the boat, hearing the pistols cracking behind them, and wondering that the time needed to cross the few yards to shore could seem like such an eternity.

His strength was nearly sapped; each time he lifted his arm in the choppy water cost him more than he could have dreamed. His breath rasped through his lungs. His knee scraped bottom and he almost shouted for joy. Pushing Robert off his back, he said, "It's yours from here, man. Get us some help, if you can."

He turned back, swimming the few feet to the boat. Grasping the bow, he stood in the water, pulling the craft about. Andrew toppled over the side, into the knee-deep water and Nicolas's supporting arms. The washerwoman tumbled out behind him. Nicolas hauled Andrew to his feet, almost carrying him as they staggered to shore.

A ball whizzed past, searing across his forehead like a flaming rod. His grunt of surprise and pain was drowned by the blast of a pistol far too close for comfort. He heard the splintering of wood, and cries of men just off shore.

His free hand automatically went to his waistband. His fingers curled around the leather pouch, clutching it as if it were the wellspring of his inner strength and determination. God, they couldn't have come this far, only to fail! He urged Andrew into a stumbling run towards the cave.

Two more staggering steps, each sending bolts of pain searing through his head, and his knees buckled beneath him. He fell to the sand, blackness threatening to overwhelm him.

"Claire!" Robert's shout came through a thick, dark fog. "Give that damned pistol over!"

Claire...? Surely not! He must be hearing things. The blackness demanded his surrender, but he wanted to grasp the most beautiful thing he'd known in his life and hold it to his heart. *Claire.* He'd only thought he'd heard her name.

Two more shots crashed in his ears, and a sudden hush descended, save for the wind and the waves. Someone was beside him, leaning over him, calling his name. His lashes flickered up, but only blood and the blurry vision of an angel met his gaze. Claire. It couldn't be. He closed his eyes, tasting the salt of tears on his lips before oblivion claimed him.

NICOLAS...stumbling, falling to the sandy beach. Claire, heart racing, grimly forced her finger round the trigger, sending a ball of lead into the side of the attacking craft. Robert's demand for her weapon met with no resistance. She shoved it into his extended hand. He fired a shot, and one of the villains toppled. He tossed the firearm aside, and Katie quickly thrust her pistol into his hand. Another neat, steady aim, and the other man fell. Claire lifted her skirts and ran to Nicolas. Katie and Robert followed in her wake.

"Nicolas! Nicolas!" Her frantic urging sounded near to hysteria to her ears. She sank to her knees, tears stinging her eyes and falling on Nicolas's face. The sight of the blood on his face and in his eyes squeezed her heart into a painful, tight ball. She sobbed, trembling with anxiety.

The cold hand of reason reached through her consciousness, and she breathed deeply, allowing logic to still her distracted mind and emotions. She must remain calm. Nicolas needed help. Unmindful of the presence of the other men, she ripped her petticoats, and tried to staunch the blood flowing from the gash on Nicolas's forehead.

"Where's the list?" Robert asked from beside her, directing his question to the other man, presumably Andrew.

"In his hand," came the weary-unto-death answer.

"The list! Is that all you can think of?" Claire cried. She grabbed the pouch from Nicolas's unresisting fingers and shoved it at Robert. "Here's your damned list!"

"Guard it with your life, m'lady," Robert muttered with a weak, lopsided grin. He put a hand to his shoulder and swayed. Katie sprang to his side, easing his unconscious path to the ground.

"Ladies," said Andrew, on his knees beside Nicolas. "I'm Andrew Marsh, Lord Rutledge. Pleased to make your acquaintance." He slid senseless to the sand.

"And I am Colette Le Duc," piped a voice nearby. "I'm the washerwoman who hid Andrew." She lifted a hand, dragging a coarse white wig off her head. Tossing it to the ground, she shook out a close-cropped mass of curls, and fell to her knees. She scooped a handful of sand, and let it slide through her fingers. Tears started in her eyes. "*Mon Dieu.* England. I made it, Maman."

Her lashes fluttered, and she melted into a graceful swoon.

CHAPTER THIRTEEN

CLAIRE AND KATIE exchanged a horrified glance. "Katie! What are we to do?" Claire cried, panic again rising to the fore. "They're all—"

"Yes, they are," Katie breathed, disbelief reigning supreme in her voice. She pulled at her petticoats, applying the torn strands to Robert's shoulder. "He's bleeding dreadfully, Claire. I wonder he had the strength to down those men—I vow I've never seen a neater aim!" Her tone held a wealth of ungrudging respect. Pressing more material to Robert's wound, she muttered, "Lord in Heaven! They can't have made it this far only to die now!"

Claire came to a swift decision. "We need help, Katie. You must go through the cave and rouse Clark. Be as quick as you can!" Katie stood and sprinted off, her feet flying over the ground.

"Hurry," Claire mumbled after her, sending a cursory glance towards Andrew. She didn't see blood on the bone-thin man, but the gaunt lines of his face told their own story. She spared a pang of sympathy for him, but he breathed, and there wasn't much she could do for him at present.

She made to tear another strip from her petticoat, found the leather pouch still gripped in her fingers and shoved it down her bodice. Another strip of fine fabric surrendered to her determined demand, and she pressed it to Nicolas's forehead. His features were pale and drawn in the feeble light. She wiped the blood from his face as best she could, biting back her tears. "Don't die, Nicolas," she whispered, smoothing his wet hair away from his face. "Please don't die."

She glanced at Robert and saw instantly that the petticoat Katie had used to bind his wound was soaked through with blood. She tore at her own, pressing the cloth to his wound. How could a few minutes seem like such an eternity?

"Hurry, Katie!" Robert looked as bad off as Nicolas, or worse. His hair lay wet and lank across his forehead. His scraggly beard and moustache looked rakish and unkempt. She smoothed back his hair, hardly believing there was a time she would have chosen him over Nicolas.

Nicolas. How she loved him. *Would Katie never return?* Had it only been but a few minutes? She breathed deeply, steeling herself for the wait.

Long moments later, what looked to be a brigade of servants, armed with lanterns and equipped with sturdy blankets, flooded through the cave.

She leapt to her feet. "Thank God! Clark, how glad I am to see you! See the men safely to the house; I'll go ahead and muster the maids to set things in order to receive them."

"The maids are already busy, m'lady," Clark assured her, dropping to his knees beside Nicolas. Colette stirred and opened her eyes. Clark frowned at her. "What is this?"

"She's the washerwoman who hid Andrew," Claire replied, shrugging at the unspoken question of why she'd returned with the men. "Colette, dear, do you feel able to walk to the house? Katie and I will help you."

Colette sat up, her wide eyes flitting from person to person. Slowly, she nodded and gained her feet with weary grace. Claire and Katie rushed to place supporting arms about her.

"Clark, have you sent for a doctor?"

"Yes, m'lady. Off with you now—we'll take care of the rest."

"Thank you, Clark. You're worth your weight in gold."

CLAIRE HOPED never to repeat the night. She consigned the fatigued Colette to Emma's capable care, and sent maids bustling to prepare rooms for their guests. Fear for Nicolas intruded as the doctor probed Robert's wound. That poor man writhed in agony, mumbling incoherently. Even Katie's face registered acute compassion. Andrew awoke and was fed hot broth by a crooning and motherly Mrs. Trumble. Nicolas lay inert, never once stirring, whilst his wound was cleaned and dressed.

The doctor left shortly after dawn instructing that Andrew be fed a light diet for a day or two, and that Nicolas and Robert be continuously watched. He couldn't say when either of them would regain consciousness, though he rather thought Robert would be invalided for a spell, and as for Nicolas, well, there was no telling with head wounds. He might come about in hours, or in days.

Claire wasn't encouraged, nor were her nerves soothed. Her stomach roiled with the upset and turmoil of the night—the fear, the blood, the darkness of death. The doctor suggested she seek her bed, and a chance glance in the mirror assured her he was right, for she looked positively haggard. Leaving strict instructions with Forsythe to waken her should Nicolas return to consciousness, she slipped between the sheets and willed herself to sleep. Nicolas couldn't possibly benefit from a wife with shattered nerves and wits.

CLAIRE OPENED HER EYES, peering past the drawn curtains to the new day beyond. The sun was high in the sky, sending a golden glow into her room. Emma puttered about, readying her clothes.

"I brought some food for your ladyship," the maid said, smiling. "Are you refreshed, or should I come back later?"

Claire sat up with a jerk. Her cramped fingers uncurled from the leather pouch. She'd taken it to bed. Robert had charged her with its care, and she hadn't known how else she might guard it more carefully.

"I'm much refreshed," she assured Emma, thinking it only a small lie. But she wanted to visit her patients, fulfil her duties as mistress of the house and plant herself at Nicolas's side. She endured an excruciatingly long half hour of her maid's ministrations, gulped a few hasty bites of food, tucked the leather pouch in her bodice and made for the connecting door.

"Forsythe, has he awoken?"

"No, m'lady."

She went to Nicolas, caressing his freshly shaven cheek with a soft, smooth stroke. He looked perfectly handsome, with his head swathed in white . . . but so vulnerable. "Let me know immediately he does. I must attend to some matters and then I'll be back to relieve you."

"Very good, m'lady."

In the hall, she met a clean and frisky washerwoman. Short auburn curls and velvety dark eyes showed promise of true beauty with proper rest and nutrition. "You look vastly different," she greeted Colette. "How old are you?"

Colette giggled. "I'm eighteen, madame. Emma made me scrub my face 'til it burned! And the lecture she gave me about wearing all that paint!" She sobered. "But it was necessary, madame. All those French soldiers never gave me a second glance."

Claire nodded slowly, unable to guess what this young lady had endured. "You're very wise, Colette. I hope your life in England is a vast improvement over France."

Colette's eyes shadowed. She inclined her head, nodded and brightened. "I daresay it will be." She paused, pressing her fingers together. "How does Lord Rutledge go on? I hoped, madame, that you might lend me your chaperonage to visit him? I know I've spent more than time enough alone with him in France, but well, I'm not an ugly washerwoman any longer."

Her dark eyes pleaded and Claire smiled. She rather thought Andrew Marsh, Lord Rutledge, was in for a shocking surprise. Taking Colette's arm she led her down the hall. "Wait here, dear. I'll see how our guest fares, and if he's able to take visitors."

"Thank you, madame."

"Call me Claire." Claire tapped on the door and entered. Awake, alert and eating, Andrew had bathed and shaved. His hair was neater, and a soft nightshirt disguised his skeletal shoulders. He was younger and far more handsome than Claire remembered.

She greeted him with a smile. "Good morning, Lord Rutledge. I trust the day finds you well."

"Ah, Lady Kenton," he responded, wiping his mouth, and pushing aside the tray. She noted he'd drained every last drop of broth and eaten every spot of soft eggs the doctor had ordered. "I keep pinching myself to assure me I'm not dead. I'm rather inclined to think I'm in heaven! Clean clothes, clean face, clean hair. Good food and a beautiful woman to greet me at my bedside. What more could a man ask for?''

Claire responded to his good-naturned grin with a warm smile. ''I'm so pleased to hear it, my lord. I congratulate you on your strength and fortitude for enduring all you have and living to tell the tale. I trust you'll make yourself at home here. Don't hesitate to call for whatever you may need.''

''Thank you, kind lady. And never fear that I shan't live it up in fine style. Mmm, just the smell of this fresh linen is enough to make me laugh! But, I say, as good as the food is, don't you suppose that nipcheese Nicolas could afford to give me a bit more?'' He gave her a wry grin.

''Doctor's orders, my lord,'' Claire said, chuckling. ''I trust you'll obey them. It's true you need some fat on your bones, but he says you must do so by careful measure, and not engorge yourself lest you become ill.''

''Yes, so he tells me. A cruel devil, if I don't miss my guess.'' He sighed, resting his head against the pillows. ''I don't think I'll ever get enough food again.''

Claire nodded sympathetically.

''But tell me, what happened to my washerwoman?'' Andrew asked. ''A good and faithful woman, that. Gave me what scraps she could afford, and kept the traitors at bay. I daresay I'd be inclined to marry her, were she thirty years younger.''

Claire could scarcely contain a laugh. He would get a shock. She felt a bit of a devil at her decision not to enlighten him. ''Well, kind sir, she awaits just outside your chamber. She wonders if you're well enough to receive visitors.''

''Well, dash it all, of course I am! Never got a chance to thank her properly.''

Claire nodded. "I'll fetch her, then." Opening the door, she ushered Colette inside. Colette shyly hung back, but Claire urged her forward. "Lord Rutledge," she introduced, keeping a sharp eye on his baffled countenance, "Colette Le Duc...your ugly old washerwoman."

Colette curtsied and Andrew peered closer, his face a picture of conflicting emotions. "But...but," he stuttered.

"I had to do it, monsieur!" Colette apologized, appearing much distressed. "You've no notion how trying it is to remain virtuous around a slew of filthy French soldiers! Not to mention my genteel birth, which made me a prime target for such swine!"

Andrew's face softened and he held out his hand. "Come closer, Colette. I may call you that, mayn't I?" She nodded, placing her hand in his. "I understand your predicament. Your deception was marvellous—brilliant! I trust it served you well?"

She nodded, a smile peeking through her blush.

He chuckled, a deep, resonant sound in the hush of the room. "You fooled me, and I lived under your roof. I'm proud of you. You're a brave young woman." He kissed her fingertips. "And kind and good, as well. Thank you."

An insistent tapping at the door sent Claire to open it. A footman bowed before her. "Beggin' your pardon, m'lady, but there's a fancy gentleman here from London insistin' he see his lordship. Clark don't know him, and as he came with an escort of armed outriders, well, Clark said as how it'd be best if m'lady spoke with him first. He said his name is Lord Renshaw."

"Lord Renshaw, you say?" Andrew asked from the bed. "Send him up...under heavy guard."

Claire remembered Nicolas's mentioning the name of Lord Renshaw. His superior? Thank God Andrew was awake to identify the man. She didn't want any trouble from anyone. She wanted to get back to Nicolas. She turned to the footman. "Lord Rutledge says to send the man up under heavy guard."

"Do call me Andrew," he said after she'd shut the door behind the footman. "And by the by, how are my rescuers today?"

"Still unconscious. I fear Robert didn't take well to having the bullet removed. A most unpleasant experience. Nicolas has a bandaged head, and we're watching for concussion. We can but wait until they regain their senses." She shrugged, impatient of every moment spent away from Nicolas.

"I'd best go," Colette told Andrew. "May I come again?"

Andrew lifted her hand to his lips. "I'd be delighted to have your company."

She smiled, nodded and left the room. The door opened almost directly behind her and a group of men filed in.

"Same old Andrew," said a man with a balding pate from the centre of a circle of several footmen. "Mayhap you'd like to tie my hands behind my back?"

Andrew studied the man. A slow smile widened his mouth. "Ah, Renshaw. A man can't be too careful."

Renshaw beamed. Claire directed the footmen away and Renshaw crossed to the bed. He grasped Andrew's hand, pumping it heartily. "Andrew, you old devil! I thought to never see you again! Dropped a few pounds, have you? I daresay you've a long story to relate!"

"I do indeed. Perhaps her ladyship will send up some tea and cakes and I'll explain the whole. By the by, have you met Nicolas's wife?"

"I haven't had the pleasure," Lord Renshaw said, turning to Claire. He bowed over her hand. "I now see why Kenton rushed to wed you. You're very lovely."

Claire blushed.

"Not only that, Renshaw," Andrew said, " but she's a fine woman. Saved our hides last night, and that's a fact. I'll tell you all about it as soon as we get those cakes."

"Eat sparingly!" Claire reminded him with a laugh. She curtsied to Lord Renshaw. "I'm pleased to meet you, my lord. But I must leave you gentlemen now as I'm anxious to return to Nicolas. I'll send a tray and if there's aught else you need, just ring."

"Thank you," Andrew said. "I daresay Nicolas won't thank me if I keep his beautiful wife at my bedside, instead of his. Thank you too, for your help on the beach last night. We never would have made it if it weren't for you and your sister. We hadn't another shot to fire. If I might say so, Nicolas is a very lucky man."

"Thank you. Oh, and would you like the list?"

"The list!" Andrew exclaimed. "Good God, yes. I've been so rejoicing in my good fortune that I quite forgot my duties." He grinned at Renshaw. "I hope you're pleased to know my mission was successful."

Renshaw clapped him heartily on the shoulder. "Dashed fine job, old man. Castlereagh will be a happy man."

Discreetly, Claire turned and removed the leather pouch from her bodice. Renshaw accepted it with a smile as wide as the Strait. "Bless you."

"It was the least I could do. I'll come by again." She lifted a hand in salute and left the room, closing the door softly behind her. She only hoped Nicolas would bless her as well, and not be angry that she'disobeyed him.

Robert's room wasn't far away, and she entered, finding the curtains drawn and the room shrouded in gloom. Katie sat at his bedside, bathing his face with a cool cloth.

"Katie, did you rest well?" asked Claire, moving up beside her. She gazed at Robert, noting the flush on his clean-shaven cheeks. "Have you breakfasted yet?"

Katie nodded. "I had Cook send up a tray, and yes, I slept well enough. However, I fear Major West didn't. Mrs. Trumble said he did not stop tossing, even when they tried to bathe him and change his linens. He's been wringing with sweat, but the doctor said the fever was expected. He's come and gone already today, leaving more laudanum."

A gleam of worry lurked in the depths of Katie's eyes, and Claire reached out, resting her hand on her sister's shoulder. "I'm sure he'll be fine, Katie. The doctor said he's in excellent physical condition. The ball did hit him from a distance, and didn't damage any vital organs."

"Oh, Claire, I feel so awful, so *guilty!* I've thought such bad things of him, but I swear I never wished him to die!"

"He won't die, Katie," Claire assured her. "Besides, you helped him gain his bed. I feel you've more than paid for any hateful things you've thought against him."

Katie sniffed and nodded. "You're right, of course. But Claire, he was in such dreadful pain last night! And only think that he remained conscious until he'd shot those men! I feared he'd die when the doctor removed the bullet—have you ever seen anything more dreadful, and knowing you can do nothing to help?"

"You mustn't dwell on it too much, dear. And do calm yourself, lest you make yourself ill. Mama won't thank me if that happens."

"Mama would swoon if she knew of my stay here!" said Katie with a watery laugh. "Why, all this bloodshed! Not to mention that I've been alone all morning in a man's bedchamber, especially when that man is Major Robert West!"

"Why especially?"

"Because he's a philanderer and a lech, that's why," Katie stated matter-of-factly. "But he's also wounded. Therefore, I believe I'm safe."

"You still think ill of him?"

"Of course. I told you I saw him with *that* woman. But, be that as it may, I daresay my reputation can stand his presence—until he mends, at any rate."

"Indeed," agreed Claire. The knowledge of Robert's perfidy had caused her little grief, but had Nicolas done the same, she surely would have been heartbroken. Thinking of Nicolas chafed her impatience. She was honour bound to fulfil her duties as hostess, but oh, how every second seemed like an hour! "I must go to Nicolas now, Katie. Do let me know if there's any change in Robert."

Nicolas's bedchamber was also shrouded in darkness. Claire crept in, sighing, thankful to be with him at last. "He hasn't awakened?"

"No, m'lady," Forsythe answered.

She frowned. "I'll stay with him. You must be fatigued."

Forsythe inclined his head and surrendered his chair. Claire settled herself into it, and gazed at Nicolas. His face was still pale, but he seemed to rest peacefully. Only the slightest stain of red showed through the bandages on his head, assuring her the bleeding had almost ceased. She lifted his limp hand and pressed it to her cheek.

She watched him steadily, content to stare at his face in repose. The bandage lent him a rakish air, his lashes fanned his cheeks and his lips looked soft and vulnerable. How she loved him! And how long it had taken her to acknowledge that truth.

The memory of their waltz at Almack's imposed itself...of her rippling fear at the thought of his offering for her. A smile touched her lips. How glad she was he had! Even if he never returned her love, she was glad to be his wife, to know his lovemaking...and she would happily bear him his heir. Several of them, if he so desired!

He was home. The danger had passed. He was safe, and would mend. And she'd stay at his side until she saw those cool grey eyes open. She wouldn't be dragged away again.

NICOLAS BROKE THROUGH the black haze surrounding him. A thousand fiends of hell taunted him. He wanted to jerk upright with a shout, but some inner caution refused him such release. Thus he lay, gradually becoming aware of his surroundings; the soft bed he lay on, and his hand...held by soft skin and against soft skin.

His eyes flickered open. Claire. A beautiful and welcome sight! His brows knotted in thought. Claire...on the beach? Leaning over him? The pistols, the shots...the salty taste of tears on his lips. What the hell? Was this his chamber? Whatever had transpired?

"Nicolas," Claire breathed, "you're awake." Her eyes glistened with unshed tears, and a smile of joy lifted her lips.

He looked round the room, and his gaze returned to her. Was this real? Or was Claire at his bedside just another dream? "We made it, then?"

He found it difficult to talk. His mouth was dry. "Water?"

"Oh, certainly!" She dropped his hand and lifted the pitcher from his bedstand. She gently raised his head, but still he winced at the throbbing pain. After he had taken several swallows, she tenderly returned his head to the pillows.

"Yes, Nicolas," she said, "you made it."

Her eyes were bright green jewels. Were those tears lurking in their depths? For whom? Robert? His gut twisted as if pierced by a dagger, but he couldn't hate the man. Envy he might, but not hate. And how were his comrades? "Andrew and West?"

"Andrew is awake and complaining about the lack of food. He calls you a nipcheese, and the doctor a cruel devil. He appears to be in high spirits. Your superior, Lord Renshaw, is visiting with him now."

"Renshaw here?" He frantically felt about his person, his hand contacting with nothing but bare skin. He grasped her wrist. "The list. Where is it?"

"I gave it to Renshaw. It's safe."

He breathed a deep sigh of relief, then shook his head. "I didn't think we'd make it. Claire...I told you to stay in the house. For God's sake, you might have been killed."

"Yes, I might have, but I wasn't. Don't be angry with me, Nicolas. I *had* to do whatever I could."

Why, he wondered, *for West?* Did it matter? She was with him now, and try as he might, he couldn't summon even a scowl of displeasure. Instead, one side of his mouth quirked up. "Thank God you did. We'd never have made it off the beach. Thank you, Claire. You saved our lives.''

She smiled and nodded, uttering a humble "It was in my best interest, my lord.''

Again, he experienced a knife sharp pain within him. His heart cursed him for loving a woman who loved another man. "How is Robert, then?''

She shook her head. "He didn't take well to having the bullet removed. He's feverish and unconscious. The doctor says we just have to wait. Katie's been with him all morning.''

He closed his eyes, remembering the hellish journey across the Strait. If he never had to travel it again, he would be happy. "And Robert shot the men in the boat?''

"Mmm. He's a neat aim.''

He nodded. Claire's fingers entwined with his, and, startled, his gaze flew to her.

"How are you feeling?'' she asked, lifting her other hand to trail across his cheek.

He closed his eyes, revelling in her touch. If only she loved him, he'd find the strength to jump to the moon. "I have a headache, my forehead burns and my arms feel like lead. But I'm glad to be alive.''

"I'm glad you are alive.''

He opened his eyes to her tender smile, and marvelled. He wanted to ask if she really meant it—

A tap came on the door. It opened to admit Renshaw. "May I come in? Ah, Nicolas, you've awakened from the dead, I see. Quite an heroic deed you men accomplished. I'm proud of you.''

Nicolas nodded, a faint smile curving his lips. "Thank you, but we never would have made it, had it not been for Claire.''

"Indeed. Damned interesting that my three top men needed to be saved by women." He chuckled. "I must be off to London with all haste, but I wanted to check on your health first. Your lovely bride gave me the list. Does Henry Bascombe, Baron Meade, sound familiar? Seems he's our English ringleader. I'll have him in irons as soon as may be, and send word when the deed is done. You got the other three, I think, so I daresay you may start breathing freely. And by the by, I rather think your spying days are done. Married man and all that."

"I should hope so!" Claire fervently declared.

Renshaw chuckled. "You have a worthy bride, Kenton."

"Thank you, Renshaw. I rather agree with you." He glanced at Claire, and she smiled at him, a bit tremulously, with a touch of wonder.

"Well," said Renshaw, "must be on my way. I'll tidy up all odds and ends—you concentrate on your recuperation. Lady Kenton, thank you for your help. And Nicolas? I'm glad it's done."

"My sentiments exactly, Renshaw. God speed."

The door shut behind him with a quiet click. Nicolas looked into Claire's eyes. After a moment, she asked softly, "Did you mean that?"

"That you're a worthy bride? Every word of it." He paused. Should he bare his heart, or continue hiding it from her? Lifting her hand, he kissed it. "Claire, I know when we married, I wanted only an acceptable wife. But that's not enough for me any more." He swallowed hard. "I love you."

There, it was out, and her eyes were shining with emotions he'd never seen in their clear green depths. Hope, wonderment...love? He had to say one more thing. "I'm aware you love West...but I hope someday to steal your affections away from him.''

Close to tears, Claire drew a deep breath and rushed into speech. "I sat at the window, waiting for your return, and I thought I'd die if you didn't. It wasn't Robert I waited for. I have been lacking in sense. And when I saw you fall..." She gulped, blinking back the tears. Lifting her head higher, she said in a stronger voice, "Nicolas, you're wonderful, and...and I love you."

Nicolas stared, amazement and a tentative spring of hope rising within him. He seized her hand, tugging her from the chair and onto the bed beside him.

"Claire." 'Twas all he could say—nothing else would pass his constricted throat. He pulled her into his arms, and held her close, cherishing the feel of her. He smoothed back her hair. "You're sure you don't love Robert West?"

"Not in the way I love you. I feel something different with you, something deeper, something more special than I have words to explain. At this moment, it is so perfect, being here in your arms—'tis the only place I ever want to be."

Nicolas studied her, loving every line of her face, every emotion apparent in her eyes. He smoothed his palm across her hair, and embraced her. "'Twas a damned beastly business, trying to find an acceptable wife, but I daresay the end of my quest has surpassed my every dream."

Claire smiled and drew closer, lifting her lips for his kiss. Bless the Earl of Kenton's handsome eyes! She remembered how, once, she would have done almost anything to avoid becoming Kenton's countess. But oh, she decided, her mouth melting against his, how she would have been cheated had she not!

Harlequin Regency® Romance ™

COMING NEXT MONTH

#77 WAYWARD ANGEL by Vivian Keith
Miss Annabelle Winthrop recognized her feelings for
Camford Singletary, the Earl of Westerbrook,
immediately. Yet he struggled to resist similar
feelings for her. Annabelle committed herself to
teaching him that it was better to have loved and lost
than never to have loved at all.

#78 BITTERSWEET REVENGE by Gail Whitiker
Miss Regana Kently had no reason to hope that she
of all ladies would attach the interest of the
"Unmarriageable Earl" of Westmorlen. And even
less expectations that he would ask her to become his
countess. Nevertheless, she was devastated to learn
of the earl's devilish scheme to marry her and kill
two birds with one stone.

Summer Reading At Its Best

In July, Harlequin and Silhouette bring readers the Big Summer Read Program. Heat up your summer with these four exciting new novels by top Harlequin and Silhouette authors.

SOMEWHERE IN TIME by Barbara Bretton
YESTERDAY COMES TOMORROW by Rebecca Flanders
A DAY IN APRIL by Mary Lynn Baxter
LOVE CHILD by Patricia Coughlin

From time travel to fame and fortune, this program offers something for everyone.

Available at your favorite retail outlet.

BSR

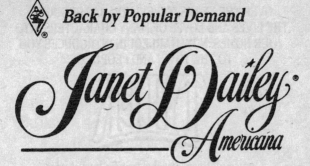

Back by Popular Demand

Janet Dailey
Americana

A romantic tour of America through fifty favorite Harlequin
Presents, each set in a different state researched by Janet
and her husband, Bill. A journey of a lifetime in one
cherished collection.

In July, don't miss the exciting states featured in:

Title #35 OHIO
The Widow and the Wastrel
#36 OKLAHOMA
Six White Horses

OVER THE YEARS, TELEVISION HAS BROUGHT
THE LIVES AND LOVES OF MANY CHARACTERS INTO
YOUR HOMES. NOW HARLEQUIN INTRODUCES YOU
TO THE TOWN AND PEOPLE OF

One small town—twelve terrific love stories.

GREAT READING...GREAT SAVINGS... AND A FABULOUS FREE GIFT!

Each book set in Tyler is a self-contained love story; together, the twelve novels stitch the fabric of the community.

By collecting proofs-of-purchase found in each Tyler book, you can receive a fabulous gift, ABSOLUTELY FREE! And use our special Tyler coupons to save on your next TYLER book purchase.

Join us for the fifth TYLER book,
BLAZING STAR by Suzanne Ellison, available in July.

Is there really a murder cover-up?
Will Brick and Karen overcome differences and find true love?

COMING IN JULY
FROM HARLEQUIN HISTORICALS

TEMPTATION'S PRICE
by Dallas Schulze

Dallas Schulze's sensuous, sparkling love stories have made her a favorite of both Harlequin American Romance and Silhouette Intimate Moments readers. Now she has created some of her most memorable characters ever for Harlequin Historicals....

Liberty Ballard...who traveled across America's Great Plains to start a new life.

Matt Prescott...a man of the Wild West, tamed only by his love for Liberty.

Would they have to pay the price of giving in to temptation?

AVAILABLE IN JULY WHEREVER HARLEQUIN BOOKS ARE SOLD